BLUE BLOOD WILL OUT

Tim Heald

A Lythway Book

CHIVERS PRESS
BATH

First published in Great Britain 1974
by
Hutchinson Publishing Group
This Large Print edition published by
Chivers Press
by arrangement with
the author
1991

ISBN 0 7451 1271 4

Copyright © 1974 by Tim Heald

British Library Cataloguing in Publication Data

Heald, Tim *1944–*
    Blue blood will out.
    I. Title
    823.914 [F]

    ISBN 0–7451–1271–4

Printed and bound in Great Britain by
REDWOOD PRESS LIMITED, Melksham, Wiltshire

BLUE BLOOD WILL OUT

Freddie, third Earl of Maidenhead, donned his custom-made swimming trunks, crossed the stately lawns of Abney House, and dived into the Thames for his morning swim. About midstream he suddenly stopped. His arms and legs went limp. He was, of course, extremely dead. Investigator Simon Bognor arrives looking for the gunman and is alarmed to find himself the target of a murder attempt. It helps the case, though not Bognor's nerves, when the list of suspects is shortened by the death of Sir Canning Abney. Bognor pokes among the remaining gentry in the search of clues, a black sheep, a motive—anything, even if it means getting too close for comfort to a wild bison hunt.

To Alison

BLUE BLOOD WILL OUT

CHAPTER ONE

The morning mist hung low over the Thames, veiling, but not wholly obscuring, the stumps of newly pollarded willow and the white bushes of hawthorn which lined the opposite bank. Two moorhens stalked each other across the impeccably manicured lawn, their heads jerking in twitchy unison, and from the house itself there sounded the howl of a discontented dog.

It was just seven. Too early for most of Sir Canning's guests to be doing much more than tossing restlessly as the sun filtered through gaps in the curtains. Stately home owners—even the most emancipated and extrovert—are not generally the earliest of risers and the select few who were attending the first annual conference of Abney Enterprises were more likely to burn midnight oil than catch worms.

The exception was Frederick, third Earl of Maidenhead. There was nothing out of the ordinary in this because the Earl prided himself on being perverse. At six-thirty he had woken, drunk one cup of Twining's Russian Caravan Tea from the Teasmade machine at his bedside and put on a pair of individually styled bathing trunks with the legend FM embroidered on the left leg. He had then made his way downstairs,

1

across the gravel, round the fountain and the floodlights, and over the grass to the cord covered springboard. At six-fifty he patted his putty-coloured paunch twice, took three deep breaths of invigorating Thames Valley air and smoothed his abundant grey locks with the palm of his right hand. He then extended both arms in front of him, bounced lightly on the board and dived. A few yards out he rose to the surface and started to crawl slowly towards Berkshire.

Now at seven he was drifting downstream and was indeed leaving the Abney land on his port side. He was almost exactly in midstream and he appeared to be making no effort to swim further. His arms and legs were perfectly limp. He was, of course, extremely dead.

*   *   *

Lord Maidenhead's demise was not allowed to interfere with breakfast for the very good reason that it was not discovered until after the meal was over. Even if it had been, the house guests would almost certainly still have breakfasted well. They were not a noticeably sentimental collection and they had not been particularly fond of the dead man. Besides they had paid for their breakfast.

The first to arrive in the dining-room, at half past eight, was the host and owner—or more

2

properly the proprietor—of Abney House, Sir Canning Abney himself. Sir Canning was remarkable if only because he had turned the business of opening a stately home to the public from a flamboyant improvisation into an exact science. When he had inherited the Abney estate from his father fifteen years before he had been advised to sell out. The income from the farms was negligible and the whole estate had been deplorably managed for a quarter of a century. There were death duties of several hundred thousand and the house was falling down. Three property developers had approached him within hours of his father's death, which had decided him. If the estate was going to make money it was going to make it for him. He had sacked the agent; sold off a minute proportion of the land for an exorbitant price; modernized the farms, evicting tenants where possible and installing managers; and most important of all opened the house to the general public and founded the 'small ships museum'. At eight-thirty that morning, as he helped himself to kidneys, Sir Canning was a happy man. The weekend conference established him as undisputed leader of the stately home industry. By an unfortunate quirk of fate, last year's attendance figures had suggested that the outrageously eccentric and inefficient Earl of Maidenhead had become leader of the league and Sir Canning had been forced to console

3

himself with the thought that he undoubtedly made less money. Now, with the conference, he was back on top.

He bisected a kidney, looked at his watch (gold from Garrards) and frowned. The first seminar—on catering—was scheduled for ten. He very much hoped there would be no backsliding.

Lady Abney breakfasted, as usual, in bed where she spent a great deal of her time, not always alone and not always with her husband; and the next arrival in the dining-room was another of Sir Canning's paying guests. He was a small, leather-skinned man with a clipped military moustache and quick ferrety movements. Late forties. He walked purposefully to the sideboard where he lifted each of the silver covers in turn before finally helping himself to two rashers of crisp back bacon and some scrambled egg.

'Morning,' said Sir Canning.

'Morning,' said the McCrum.

'Sleep well?'

'Very. Overslept I'm afraid.' The McCrum picked up a copy of the *Daily Telegraph* and turned to the sports page.

'It's the air,' said Abney. 'Very soporific. Takes you two days to get used to it.'

The McCrum grunted. He had not wished to come south on this gimmick-ridden jaunt, much less spend a hundred guineas for the privilege, but as the owner of Scotland's most flamboyant castle he had felt it proper. Or, more accurately, Lady Mabel had thought it proper. She was upstairs titivating.

'Anybody else about?' asked Sir Canning.

'Passed old Lydeard in the corridor. Fellow was muttering about Alka Seltzer.'

Conversation now ceased. Sir Canning had toast with home-made marmalade. He had banned Frank Cooper's on the grounds that the quantity of orange peel in it had diminished. The McCrum turned to the Peterborough column.

Gradually the room filled until everyone was there with the exception of Lady Abney, the Earl and Countess of Maidenhead and Peter Williams, the agent and managing director of Abney Enterprises. Sir Canning drank coffee from a vast, elaborately patterned cup and looked round with pleasure. There were, he conceded, absentees. No Marquis of Bath, no Montagu of Beaulieu, no Bedford, but by and large the gathering was impressive.

'No sign of the Maidenheads?' asked Sir Canning, addressing the company at large.

The Marquis of Lydeard, mouth full of sausage, shook his head briefly and Mr Cosmo Green, the new owner of Hook, shrugged expressively. He was there to advise about money, which he was good at. Sir Canning looked at the far end of the table and raised his

5

eyebrows. 'Tony?' he enquired. The Hon. Anstruther Grithbrice said 'No' and turned to his neighbour, a voluptuous black girl, whom he had introduced the night before as Honeysuckle Johnson. 'Have you, Honey?' he asked.

'Not a sign,' she said in a husky Eartha Kitt voice.

'Oh,' Sir Canning grimaced and got up. 'If,' he said, 'any of you should bump into them you might remind them that we have catering at ten. In the boardroom.' He put *The Times* under his arm and walked out.

Outside in the dark corridor he almost ran into his butler. 'I'm sorry, sir,' said Mercer. 'I was just coming for you. Mr Williams is on the phone.'

'The phone?' Sir Canning's satisfaction was jolted. Peter Williams had a flat in the house, over the old stables. It had its own entrance but it wouldn't have taken him more than thirty seconds to walk round. Besides he invariably had breakfast in the main dining-room.

'I'll take it in the office,' he said irritably. 'Did he sound all right? Not ill?'

'No, sir. Not at all.'

'Good. He'd better not be.' He opened the green baize-covered door which separated the private sector of his home from the public, stepped lightly over a purple rope barrier, across the great hall with its seascapes and

6

engraved oars, coats of arms and photographs of admirals and rowing eights, and opened another door, in a far corner, marked 'Private'. This was the office block, much of it a recent addition built out into a courtyard where no one could see it.

'Morning, Miss Adams,' he said to his private secretary, a thin-faced spinster in her late thirties. 'I'll deal with this and then we'll do the mail straight away. We have a full day today.'

'Good morning, Sir Canning. Yes, of course.'

He went past her and into his office beyond, where he sat down heavily in the high-backed revolving leather armchair and flicked a switch on the long slim silver and black device on the desk. 'Peter?' he said, leaning back in the chair.

'Hello, yes, it's me.' The voice sounded oddly real even after the amplication. It was an expensive system—Danish. 'I'm afraid we've had a slight accident.'

'Oh Christ.' Sir Canning was peeved. 'Not now of all times,' he said. 'What is it?'

'Not serious,' said Williams. 'It's just that I took Lady Maidenhead out for a spin in the *Charlotte* last night and we broke down.'

'Broke down?'

'It's all right. She's fixed now. It's just that we'll both be a bit late. Lady Maidenhead's rather distressed. Could you explain to her husband?'

'He's not down yet. Anyway it's your

problem not mine. You'll have to explain for yourselves. When will we see you?'

'About a quarter of an hour. I'm at a phone box in Marlow.'

'O.K. Quarter of an hour.'

Sir Canning flicked the switch back and pursed his lips. Miss Adams came in with a bundle of letters and he smiled at her, wryly. 'I do hope,' he said, 'we're not going to have trouble.'

CHAPTER TWO

Lady Maidenhead, it was generally agreed, received the news of her husband's death with disquieting equanimity. The announcement was made by a policeman who arrived on a motor bike ten minutes before the seminar on catering was due to begin. The body, he told Sir Canning, had been washed up at Cookham Weir and spotted by a man out walking his dog. The police had recognized the dead man from photographs in the press, and confirmed his identity from the initials on his bathing trunks. He said nothing about the cause of death but concluded lamely that somebody else would be coming later.

'I was sent to tell you and her ladyship as quickly as possible,' he said. 'We knew they were staying here. Read it in William Hickey.' He twisted the immense gauntlets in his hands and smiled nervously. 'Could I see her ladyship?'

'I think perhaps it would be more ... er ... appropriate if I told her myself,' said Sir Canning. He dismissed the policeman, instructed Mercer to prepare a ritual glass of brandy and buzzed the boardroom.

'Peter? Is Lady Maidenhead there?'

'Everyone's here.'

'I'll be right up. Warn her I want a word in private, would you?'

Upstairs, Lady Maidenhead refused to have a word in private. After Sir Canning had made his little speech she drank the brandy before remarking, 'Silly old twit. I told him not to bring his trunks. He's not used to fresh water.' She then asked for a second brandy.

The Earl had been more than twenty years her senior, and their marriage, which had been his second, had lasted five years. In that time her extravagant good looks had wilted but not faded away completely. The other guests seemed, more predictably, to be embarrassed rather than anguished with the possible exception of Mabel McCrum who went rather white and dabbed surreptitiously at her eyes with a small lace handkerchief. However in view of Lady Maidenhead's refusal to do the decent thing and have hysterics there was

9

nothing for it but to continue, albeit nervously, with the session on catering.

It was introduced by Sir Canning. He spoke succinctly, disclaiming any great responsibility for the growth of his restaurant and cafeteria business from the original small tea shop to the massive pre-cooked infra-red operation which he now controlled. On a good day now they sold over a thousand pounds' worth of chips and lollies and baked beans as well as scampi *á la mode d'Abney* to the more discerning in 'The Cabin' restaurant. After five minutes he made way for Peter Williams.

Williams, it was immediately clear to his listeners, was a technocrat. He was wearing what Americans used to call an Ivy League suit and he illustrated his talk with slides. The McCrum, who sat next to the Marquis of Lydeard, leant across and whispered in his ear 'Slough Grammar and Harvard Business School if you ask me.' Lydeard chortled obligingly and Sir Canning said 'Shhhh'. Williams spoke for half an hour, allowing the catering manager, an oily person in his early thirties, who had been poached from his job running a motorway service station, to say a very few words.

The theme of the lecture was profitability without waste. Abney Enterprises employed pigs as refuse disposal units. 'Ecological chain,' said Williams. 'Human waste in the form of unfinished meals is fed to our pigs and the pigs

10

are fed back to the public in pork pies. It's biologically perfect and it involves total maximization of profit.'

There were other ways in which he saved and therefore made money. 'This,' he said, showing a slide of a long queue of trippers, 'involves waste and dissatisfaction, but so ...' and he switched to a slide showing no queues at all, 'does this. There is an optimum speed for consumer traffic. Push your customer through too fast and he is irritable and spends too little money. He won't have any afters and he won't have a second cup of coffee. Push him through too slowly and,' he switched back to the previous slide, 'you get this. Customers waiting and maybe even being turned away and going elsewhere for their meals. Your lucky client who's got his food may spend more because he's allowed to linger; but no amount of extra buying by the few can compensate for money spent by the many. You have to strike a happy mean. Everyone has to feed well and expensively. Not too expensively. Nobody must feel he's spent more than he can afford or he'll feel cheated and he won't come back. But we have to get to the highest possible profit level below that figure.'

Sir Canning had been showing signs of restiveness. 'Thank you, Peter,' he said, 'for such a lucid exposition. There's just one point I would like to emphasize.' He stuck a hand in his jacket pocket and tried to look affable. 'Although of course we are in the business to make money there is no substitute for quality. We here at Abney have very few complaints and the reason for that is that we supply, as the public would have it, "first-rate nosh". You'll have an opportunity to see for yourselves over the weekend but I can't say too forcefully that we would never dream of taking on an outside caterer, simply because by doing so we lose control over the quality of our food and drink.' He paused and peered round beaming, trying to see whether he had re-established his philanthropic credentials. 'Right,' he said. 'Thank you again, Peter. I'll throw it open now. Any questions or observations, anyone?'

'Yes.' It was Anstruther Grithbrice. 'We've always used outside people at Netherly,' he drawled, 'and I agree that they're a pretty fearful lot but they do save us a lot of fag *and* we have a guaranteed income. I mean they pay a set amount every year. Why involve yourself in a hell of a risk and a hell of a lot of hard work when you can get someone else to do it for you?'

'I'm afraid,' Sir Canning was looking patronizing, 'that success in this field does involve both risk and hard work. Unless perhaps,' he smiled icily, 'you're lucky enough to have quite such a magnificent attraction as Netherly.'

'I must say I had a rotten lunch in your

cafeteria, Grithbrice,' said the McCrum. 'Not even hot.'

'You should have told us you were coming, instead of snooping round incognito. Then you could have had a proper lunch with us. Serves you right for being shifty.'

'I always maintain,' said Lydeard, 'that the public either comes to see me or the bison or the Canalettos. I don't know that they really want more than a good cup of tea.'

'I always say sod the public,' said Grithbrice, 'and talking of tea, what about coffee?' The coffee was in fact waiting and the meeting split into small groups, each one discussing the relative merits of different sorts of packaging, of different ice-cream companies, fixed seating, plastic cups and gratuities. Before long, however, the individual conversations took a gloomier turn.

'Poor old Maidenhead,' said Lydeard, who seldom intentionally spoke ill of anyone, least of all the dead. 'Frightfully upsetting for poor Eva. Can't think what possessed him to go larking about in the river at that time of the morning, I suppose he got cramp.'

'She doesn't look upset,' said the McCrum, and the two stared towards the window by which the newly bereaved Countess was sitting, talking animatedly to an attentive Peter Williams. 'If you ask me,' continued the Scot, 'there's something going on there. And as for

Maidenhead he was a charlatan and a mountebank and we all know it. He gave the aristocracy a bad name.'

'Oh I say,' said Lydeard, 'fellow's only just dead, y'know.'

Over by the fireplace, Grithbrice, his girl friend, and Sir Canning had also forgotten the problems of feeding the public and were debating the consequences of the fatality.

'Awkward,' Grithbrice was saying. 'It can't help casting rather a blight over the ceremony. The papers are going to be a little muted in their enthusiasm.'

'Awkward's the word,' agreed Sir Canning. 'If only he could have waited till Monday and done it at home. He spent all his life trying to bugger me up and now he's continuing after he's died. It really is tiresome of him.'

'You English,' said Miss Johnson, who had a Ph.D. in Contemporary Communications from a little known university in Idaho, 'are lacking in sensitivity.'

The two men took united umbrage. 'Not in the least,' said Sir Canning. 'We just conceal our emotions. Certain things are better left unexpressed, and grief is one of them.'

'Always sounds mawkish,' said Grithbrice.

Near the door Mr Green, who was short, swarthy and good-looking in a short, swarthy way, was standing between Lady Abney and Lady McCrum. The two women were arguing over the top of Mr Green's head. Mr Green watched and listened in the disinterested manner of an umpire at Wimbledon.

'But, darling,' said Lady Abney, 'we just have to go on. We can't possibly cancel every single invitation. There's the press and the tea's all ordered. It's simply not fair on Canning. Besides we can't afford it.' She was in her early fifties, scrupulously neat in tweed suit from either a select mail order business or one of the smarter London stores. Like Lady McCrum she wore pearls.

'I still think it's quite wrong,' said Lady McCrum, 'I appreciate that it involves you in a certain amount of inconvenience but it's the least you can do. I know neither of you cared for Freddie but he's dead now. I think you owe him a little respect. Don't you, Mr Green?'

Mr Green appeared startled at being addressed. He thought for a moment and then said, 'I think the Earl would have wanted the show to go on, and anyway I've always made it a rule never to let pleasure interfere with business.'

Before either of the women could question him on this curious remark there was a knock at the door and Mercer entered in the discreet and yet totally obtrusive manner of the well-trained servant. He made very little noise and his movements were tidy to the point, almost, of non-existence. And yet within a moment of his

15

arrival conversation had ceased and everyone was looking at him. He went straight to Sir Canning and said softly but distinctly, 'There's another person here from the police, sir. Quite senior I should say. He says it's important.'

Sir Canning frowned. 'Show him up,' he said.

A minute later there was another knock and Mercer came in with a weary, grey-haired, grey-suited and almost grey-faced man whom he announced as Inspector Smith.

'Ah,' Sir Canning advanced, hand outstretched. At embarrassing or inconvenient moments he was always able to retreat behind an inbred wall of charm and good manners. He introduced Inspector Smith to the assembled guests and offered coffee and a cucumber sandwich. The policeman accepted the coffee and declined the sandwich.

'Might I have a word with you, sir?' he inquired as the room murmured with a stilted attempt at normal conversation.

'If you insist. On the other hand, I suspect that we should all hear whatever it is that you have to say. We were all friends and colleagues of Lord Maidenhead. This has been a very sad and tragic loss for us all. Tragic. Truly tragic.'

'Of course, sir,' the Inspector looked at the floor and coughed in an attempt to appear respectful and sympathetic. 'Very well,' he paused. 'All your guests arrived last night, did they, sir?'

'They did.'

'Ah. Well. Perhaps it might be as well if I could say a few words to the assembled company.' He took a large white handkerchief from his trouser pocket and wiped coffee stains from his upper lip. Sir Canning, meanwhile, clapped his hands to attract attention—a superfluous gesture since every moment of their brief conversation had been monitored by everyone present.

'Ladies and gentlemen,' Sir Canning disliked having to address a gathering of intimate colleagues and rivals so formally, but he felt it was what the policeman wanted. Or needed. 'Ladies and gentlemen. Inspector Smith of the local constabulary would like a few words if you'll honour him with your attention.'

Everyone turned, cups and saucers held in just such a way as to indicate attentiveness. Inspector Smith regarded them briefly and then said, rapidly and without expression, 'Ladies and gentlemen, I regret having to follow bad news with worse, but I have to tell you that the late Earl of Maidenhead did not die of natural causes but was shot through the head with a .22 rifle, and that in consequence I am compelled to assume that the deceased was murdered by a person or persons yet unknown.'

CHAPTER THREE

Simon Bognor's day began with a boiled egg and a call from the office. It was a long and one-sided telephone conversation but more cheerful than usual. Since his not wholly successful conduct of the Beaubridge Friary affair Bognor had been assigned to strictly routine duties. Parkinson had put him back on codes, ciphers and protocol and no one could pretend that this was interesting or amusing work. Today's was a protocol mission and it was, at least, a day out. 'The Umdaka of Mangolo,' said Parkinson, 'commonly known as George, is passionate about boats. I'll have a word with Canning Abney myself to tell him he'll have to look after George for a day, and I'll tell him you're coming down to arrange it. O.K.?'

Bognor smiled to himself. Life in the special investigations department of the Board of Trade had its moments. It did not, he supposed, rate as high as MI5 or 6, but it was much more anonymous, often as exciting, and sometimes as important. Bognor had arrived in the department by mistake and stayed by default. However, even he felt capable of smoothing the path of the Umdaka of Mangolo.

'O.K.'

'Now. George will be bringing two of his wives, three security men of his own, a cook and the ambassador...' Parkinson continued with an encyclopedic briefing on the man and his country, which Bognor punctuated with toast-muffled affirmatives. Eventually he put the phone down, dressed in a tweed suit appropriate to stately home life and went downstairs to collect the Mini. By nine-thirty he was threading slowly down the Cromwell Road in the direction of the Hammersmith Flyover and Abney House.

At Slough he turned off the motorway, just past the sewage works and then took the back roads under the main railway line, through Taplow, past Nashdom Abbey, the Canadian Army Memorial Hospital, the 'Feathers', the main entrance to Cliveden, and then turned left down the narrow Hedsor Hill with the oddly named 'Garibaldi' pub and Bourne End Nurseries. At the main road he turned right towards the village and Abney itself.

He had decided to do some incognito snooping, rather as the McCrum had done at Netherly. For an hour or so he would take his place in the throng of day trippers who tripped round Sir Canning's estate to the tune of half a million twenty-five pence a year. That, he reflected with envy, represented an annual income of £125,000 before you started assessing all the extra admission charges, the souvenirs, the ice-creams and the candy floss. It was a lot of money.

Half a mile from the house he slowed the car down to join the back of the queue, which was crawling towards the automatic main barriers. There were four, rather like the entrance to an underground car park. You had to stop for a ticket which you surrendered on departure. The four barriers were ample to deal with the traffic flow but Sir Canning had no jurisdiction over the approach roads and the council had always looked on the commercialization of the house with extreme disfavour. They had refused to help with signposting, road widening, planning permission or anything else. They much preferred the refined, old-fashioned approach of the National Trust up the road at Cliveden and thought the exuberant razzmatazz of Abney inappropriate for the area. Their ob-structiveness was short-sighted and had resulted in appalling traffic problems of miles of queue throughout the year. Almost every month some official body or other would deliver a protest to Abney Enterprises who would then blandly reply that it was none of their business. In fact, Sir Canning rather approved of the hot dusty wait which his visitors had to endure. It increased his sale of soft drinks and ices.

After ten minutes Bognor was through the barriers and had squeezed the Mini into a space in the park, skilfully camouflaged behind a row

20

of poplars. The next step in the Abney plan was to put the cars below ground, but the council, perversely, was as usual fighting the idea all the way. He got out and consulted the sign-post. 'Abney House', 'Cabin Restaurant', 'Self Service Cafeteria', 'Shooting Gallery', 'Small Ships Museum', 'Conveniences', 'Excursions' . . .

His glance stuck on 'Shooting Gallery', about which he vaguely remembered adverse comments when it had opened five years before. It was during the period of the great safari park boom. Abney, he recalled, had had neither the inclination nor the space to join the competition. Instead he had argued that, conservationists apart, the average English person looked upon the lion, the buffalo and the tiger not as beautiful animals to be admired from behind barbed wire but as an amusing target to be hunted. This cynical attitude had earned him brickbats from the World Wildlife Fund, the *Ecologist* and a coterie of progressive, high-minded, international fashion models; but his judgement had been correct. In his shooting range he provided his guests with a rifle and five rounds of ammunition and invited them to take shots at lifelike moving replicas of the sorts of wild animal which now cluttered the parks of his rivals. The popular press had treated the idea as an agreeable joke, all the more so when, a year after its inauguration, he had added new targets. It then became possible not only to fire at papier mâché models of the lions of Longleat or the bison of Lydeard but also at the noble Marquises who owned them. Again he had been pilloried, this time on grounds of taste, but once more his commercial instincts had proved sound.

Bognor found himself at the back of a queue again, but this time it was a short one. A large hoarding showed a Davy Crockett figure pointing a massive hunting rifle at a herd of buffalo. Underneath, the legend was: 'The Real Safari: five shots for 50p. Money back for five kills.' A few yards further on another sign showed the heads of five leading stately home owners mounted on targets. The words were: 'Knock some chips off the old blocks. A real test of skill.'

Behind the turnstile an elderly man, in the gold and blue livery of the Abneys, sat taking fifty-pence pieces. Behind him there was a notice, the equivalent of the small print at the bottom of a contract, which said: 'Warning— Abney Enterprises can accept no liability whatsoever for any damage to life, limb or property, howsoever . . .' Bognor couldn't read any further but he knew what it was: a nasty little disclaimer which wouldn't hold water in court but which would effectively stop anyone suing for damages.

'Thank you, sir.' The old man took his

money and gave him five small silver and gold bullets which he took from a large box under the window. 'There you are, sir. Mind where you point the gun. Can't be too careful, can we, sir?'

It was quite dark inside the range, except for where the targets raced across, twenty-five yards away at the other end of the building. Bognor smelt the warm mixture of oil and spent bullets and was suddenly transported back to a similar, though less lavish range at Bovington Camp in Dorset. He'd been there with a party from the school corps. Just in front of him three prone figures, two youths and a girl in tight white jeans were firing ineffectually at the procession of giraffes and lions and peers of the realm which danced across the stage in their sights. The attendant reminded him of Bovington Camp, too. 'Squeeze the trigger . . . Squeeeeeeeze . . . don't jerk it or you won't hit a monkey's fanny in a coconut shy.' Bognor hadn't met the phrase before, but it had a nostalgic ring to it.

'Right now.' The sergeant-major figure turned to Bognor. 'Got your ammo? Right. Ever fired one of these before?'

He nodded. 'Not for a long time though.'

The sergeant-major rattled the bolt a couple of times and handed him the rifle still smoking slightly and warm to the touch. 'Right then. We'll soon see. Take your time. Five shots.'

Bognor drew back the bolt, inserted a single round, and pulled the butt into his shoulder. The ground was hard against his stomach. He looked along the barrel and watched for a moment as the succession of animals and peers rattled across his line of fire. Then he swung the barrel to the right and waited. He had decided to shoot the people rather than the animals. It somehow seemed more British.

The first owner out through the trap was a Scotsman, unrecognizable unless by his kilt. Bognor brought the barrel up, moved it ahead of the flying Scot and squeezed.

'You're too high, number three,' said the sergeant-major's voice behind him. 'Far too high. Don't pull it.'

He flicked back the bolt a little clumsily and watched the spent round fly out. Inserting the other he tried to remember the different right angles his body was supposed to make, but he had had no occasion to use a rifle recently and had, quite simply, forgotten. His next selected target looked like the Duke of Devonshire. He squeezed, more gently this time and had the satisfaction of seeing his Grace swing back abruptly and disappear from view.

'That's better, number three,' said the sergeant-major. 'First time we've had him down this morning.' The next two shots were two peers he didn't recognize. One, a stereotype in ermine, could have been anyone. He hit him

24

neatly, square in the middle of the forehead. The one after was a man in deerstalker and sideboards, whom he missed.

'Too high again, number three.' The sights, thought Bognor, who for obvious reasons always blamed his tools, were miles out. He settled down again, reminding himself to aim low and left. The first man out from the right was familiar. It was the Marquis of Lydeard. Poor old Lydeard, he thought. He waited until he was almost gone again, shot, and saw him collapse silently just as he left the stage.

He got to his feet and brushed himself down. 'Thanks,' he said, handing the rifle back to the attendant. 'You want to do something about those sights, don't you? They're high and to the right if you ask me.'

'Well, I'm not asking you.' The sergeant-major looked at him evenly. 'Nothing wrong with the sights. No complaints from anyone else. And, any case, I check them myself every morning. It's your shooting what's wrong. Not that you're bad. Just rusty, I should say. Pity to go blaming the sights.'

Bognor wasn't going to make an issue of it. He went out into the daylight. It was still bright and there were hordes of people, lying in the grass, stripped off to the waist. Candy floss and ice-creams were doing well, and a cacophony of transistor radios blared out across the grounds. From somewhere downstream the shrill toot of

25

one boat's siren was answered by the more drawn-out and deeper groan of another's. It was almost lunchtime but before venturing over to the private apartments he decided to have a look at the museum. He retraced his steps and looked at the signpost. Thirty yards and another fifteen pence later he stood gazing at a five times life size blow-up of a Victorian photograph of 'Admiral Sir Canning Abney, 1st Baronet, 1803–1901'. And underneath were the words from *The Wind in the Willows*, 'Believe me, my young friend, there is nothing, absolutely nothing, half so much worth doing as simply messing about in boats.' Bognor wondered if the hero of Besika Bay would have been happy at the juxtaposition, let alone the overall commercialization of his old seat. If he hadn't been buried at sea he would doubtless be turning in his grave.

However the museum was, in its way, magnificent. Bognor was not particularly interested in boats, let alone messing about in them, but he appreciated the airy, spacious, glass-filled structure. It opened out into an artificial basin full of water which was joined to the Thames itself by a narrow creek some forty yards long. In the water a myriad craft were moored. They were of enough variety to stir even Bognor's landlocked spirit, though many, he supposed, were merely fibreglass reconstructions. There was a Brazilian jangada, a Ceylonese catamaran and a flying proa of the sort first described by Captain Cook. An aboriginal bark-covered canoe rocked gently astern of a Severn river coracle and an Irish curragh, and just ahead of two dhows from the Persian Gulf—a Begala and a Sambuk, rigged with settee sails. Turkish caiques, two sailed sandals, a Taka and a cekterne jostled a dahabeah and a gaiasse from the Nile and an obsolete Venetian tapo. More homespun styles included dories and Labrador whalers, a Block Island boat, a No Man's Land boat from North America, and such British varieties as the Deal Galley punt, the coble, the Fifie Skiff and the Shetland Severn. In the building on dry land there were small-scale models—one of the Lake Champlain Revolutionary War gunboat *Philadelphia*, the original of which was in the Smithsonian; another of Chichester's *Gypsy Moth*.

He stood for a few moments looking at the absurd boat in which the Norwegians, Haroo and Samuelson, rowed the Atlantic in 1897, and paused also to stare at the one in which Oxford rowed the Channel in 1885. Interspersed with the boats themselves were charts and maps and trophies; photographs of Nickalls and Kelly, Beresford and Davidge; a life-sized effigy of Sir Francis Chichester; a terrible oil painting of Sir Max Aitken and Edward Heath, arm-in-arm; a reconstruction of the Lord Mayor's procession of 1454; a facsimile of Doggett's Coat and Badge; and a children's corner which included a stuffed owl and a stuffed pussycat.

The crowds were considerable without being overpowering. Many of Sir Canning's visitors, guessed Bognor, would be swarming through the cafeteria, but the ones who weren't circulated here, slowly viewing each item with open-mouthed blankness. There were no guided parties except by arrangement but there was an illustrated brochure (thirty-five pence), machines with earphones which gave you a few seconds of pre-recorded information (ten pence) and uniformed attendants of varying degrees of erudition (free). Bognor wandered over to one. He had noticed that a large section of the museum was sealed off behind a partition marked 'Private', and also that some of the craft lying at anchor in the basin were invisible under tarpaulin covers. He asked for an explanation.

'That's the steam,' came the reply.

'Steam?'

'Steam. Opened tomorrow. By the captain of the *Queen Ann*.'

'Ah.' It hadn't dawned on Bognor until that moment that all the boats on show were hand or sail propelled.

'Why isn't it advertised?' he asked.

'Only open to VIPs and Press. Public aren't allowed in.'

'What exactly is going to be opened?'

'Like I said,' the man was boorish and not over-bright, 'steam. That section in there, that's all the models. Then the real boats are out there in the harbour.'

Bognor nodded. 'What sort of boats are they? Anything new? Special? Exciting?'

'That would be telling, wouldn't it?' The man was arch, with his stupidity. 'Tell you what though.' He took Bognor by the elbow and propelled him towards the water's edge. 'See that.' He pointed towards the largest piece of floating tarpaulin, directly opposite the Fifie Skiff and the Shetland Severn.

'Yes.'

The man lowered his voice. 'That's the big attraction. Cost him thousands, that did.'

'What is it?'

'It's the *Lysander*.'

'But what is it?'

'Steam pinnace, that's what it is. Built for the Grand Duke Leopold. Almost a hundred years old.' They stared at the bulging canvas for a moment. It made Bognor feel oddly uneasy and he wished he knew why. Then with a twinge of conscience he remembered George Mangolo and looked at his watch. One o'clock. 'Christ,' he thought, 'I'd better go and do some work.'

★　　★　　★

It took him time to negotiate the barriers, guard

29

dogs and the general paraphernalia of security which shielded the baronet and his private life from his paying guests, so that when he finally effected an entrance he thought he detected a faint frisson of disapproval from the butler. Mercer came as near as a well-trained butler can to sneering. 'You are expected . . . sir,' he said, regarding the tweed suit with hauteur. 'Her ladyship is in the mauve room, and there is a telephone call.'

'Oh.' Bognor was nonplussed, as usual, by servants, however servile. 'Ah. Perhaps I'd better deal with the phone call first,' he said, and realized as he said it that he had done the wrong thing.

'Her ladyship *is* waiting,' said Mercer, icily managing to convey the notion that Lady Abney had been waiting for the better part of the week. 'Oh, yes,' said Bognor, 'of course. I'm most frightfully sorry. Lead on.'

'This way, sir.'

The mauvest thing about the mauve room was the immense display of lilac on the important Georgian sofa table in the middle of the room. Lady Abney had been sitting in front of it, drinking whisky out of a heavy glass goblet and reading *Harpers*. As Bognor was announced she got to her feet and advanced on him with extended hand. He just had time to take in the cut of the suit, the precision with which the make-up had been applied, and the

30

tell-tale age lines round the neck and eyes, when she was upon him. '*Mister* Bognor,' she said enthusiastically. 'How awfully good of you to come. I do hope you had a comfortable journey. Were you held up by the crowds? The crowds are a perfect menace at this time of year, but then they are our bread and butter, aren't they, so we mustn't complain. Would you like a drink? I do hope you haven't eaten. I've booked a table in the Cabin for the two of us. I hope you won't mind lunching *à deux*. My husband apologizes but he's simply too tied up with this wretched business conference and then,' a light wrinkle of irritation crossed her face, 'we've had this bother over Freddie Maidenhead. But still, never mind. There's no need to worry you over that, is there?' She had, without waiting for any observation on the matter of drink, poured Bognor a very stiff whisky indeed and topped up her own with a generous measure.

'Do come and sit down,' she went on, patting the sofa, 'and before we start talking about the Umdaka, do tell me, are you any relation of Humphrey Bognor?'

Sir Humphrey Bognor was an honorary herald at the College of Arms, and wrote popular books on genealogy. Simon thought him a dreadful bore and had met him only once. He was some sort of cousin and he was always being asked if he was related. Particularly by people with social pretensions. 'I'm afraid not,' he said, sipping at his khaki drink, 'at least not a close relation.' He had noticed the disappointment on Lady Abney's face and was relieved to see it clear after he had claimed some kinship with Sir Humphrey.

'I'm sorry if I'm here at an inconvenient moment,' he said. 'It's pretty routine, though. It shouldn't take long. It's just to make sure that no one takes a pot shot at poor old George Mangolo on his trip over here.' He coughed nervously, when he noticed that Lady Abney was looking slightly pained. 'Did I gather there was a phone call for me?' he asked.

'I'd almost forgotten,' said Lady Abney, screwing up her nose in the manner which had won her so many admirers as a débutante, a quarter of a century earlier. 'A Mr Parkinson from your office. I understand he sounded rather excited. I suggest you telephone him from the Cabin.'

The Cabin, at which they arrived a few minutes later, was the prestige section of the Abney catering operation. The main cafeteria was a long low building screened from the railway bridge, over which the train called the 'Marlow donkey' rumbled every half hour, by a line of weeping willows. The Cabin was on top, a penthouse affair with portholes. Most of the cafeteria roof was given over to roof garden, and after he and Lady Abney had threaded their way through a maze of tubs and trellises they

32

were greeted at the door of the restaurant by a middle-aged man in what Bognor took to be the uniform of a mid-nineteenth-century merchant navy captain. He carried sheaves of glossy menus and smelt strongy of cheap scent. There followed a prolonged and embarrassing ceremony of introduction and ingratiation after which Lady Abney was conducted to a table in the window and Bognor escaped to the phone.

'Where the bloody hell have you been?' said Parkinson when he got through.

'Looking round for threats to the safety of the esteemed George, Umdaka of Mangolo,' said Bognor lightly.

'Don't get funny with me,' said Parkinson viciously. He had had to cancel an attractive lunch date in order to wait for his subordinate to phone back and he was even now halfway through a plate of greasy steak and chips from the canteen. 'I take it you've heard by now?'

'Heard? Heard what?' Bognor was apprehensive.

There was a pause during which Parkinson could almost be heard counting to ten. Then he started to talk in the very soft tight tones which Bognor dreaded. 'I'm sorry that you haven't heard yet,' he said. 'It does seem a little strange that you haven't heard yet since practically half Britain seems to have heard now. But then, of course, you're only on the scene where it happened so I suppose you could hardly be

33

expected . . . oh, well, never mind. The Earl of Maidenhead's dead.'

'Oh,' said Bognor, cautiously. 'So?'

There was another even longer pause. Eventually Parkinson said, through what sounded like clenched teeth, 'So it's a case of murder and it interests me.'

'In what sense? He wasn't exacty politically involved. It was only Tory whist drives and things, surely?'

'You're forgetting one international situation where Tory whist drives represent pretty high-powered diplomacy,' said Parkinson, not altogether sarcastically, 'and you're also forgetting that the late Earl of Maidenhead was the proud holder of the Distinguished Flying Cross, and now surely even you . . .'

'Oh, all right,' said Bognor, 'so he was involved in Rhodesia . . .'

'Right. So he was involved in Rhodesia. So he was shot before his early morning dip. So I'm interested.'

'Oh,' said Bognor. 'Well, what do you want *me* to do about it?'

'Do what you're bloody paid to do.' Parkinson's patience had finally gone. 'Use your fucking initiative.'

Bognor was about to remonstrate when he realized that the phone had gone dead. He returned to Lady Abney humming abstractedly.

'I've taken the liberty,' she said, smiling

widely, 'of ordering lobster and a bottle of chablis. I do hope you don't mind. Jules says the lobsters are fresh in from Galway and the chablis comes from Ernest Marples.'

'Oh. Good.' Bognor picked up a roll and noticed that there was a glass of whisky in front of each plate. 'You didn't tell me,' he said, 'that you'd had an ... er ... accident this morning.'

Lady Abney smiled again and put a finger to her lips. 'Please,' she said, *'pas devant les domestiques,'* and laughed, a little too gaily.

Bognor frowned. 'I'm sorry,' he said, 'but it is rather important. I mean he was...'

'Not another word, Mr Bognor—Simon, isn't it? Not another word. I'm quite sure that my husband will want to discuss it with you. As far as I'm concerned I know nothing whatever about it. Nothing whatever.' She waved a dismissive hand in the direction of the river. 'And now,' she said, 'about the Umdaka's visit. Canning and I were wondering if he might like to arrive by canoe. It would make such wonderful photographs.'

'Paddling himself, I suppose,' said Bognor.

Lady Abney raised her eyebrows and smiled at her guest with old-fashioned radiance. 'Oh, Simon,' she said, 'I do believe you're rather a tease.'

The lobster and chablis were both excellent and Bognor was vaguely conscious not only that he and Lady Abney were getting a good deal more attention than any of their fellow lunchers, but also a great deal better food. A few of them were upper-class trippers, some were lower-class trippers who had wandered in by mistake and were too embarrassed to leave; a very few were businessmen from Wycombe and Slough. Most of them appeared to be eating scampi followed by steak. Throughout the meal his hostess refused, despite many efforts, to make any comment at all about the demise of the Earl. Apart from a great deal of badinage, of a rather forced sort, she remarked only that 'Old Freddie was all right in his way.' She also told Simon that one of the house guests was Anstruther Grithbrice's latest, a sexy black girl called Johnson. Bognor wondered if she might have anything to do with the crime. If there was a political motive she seemed to be the only person who was even remotely likely.

Eventually, after declining port, brandy or Gaelic coffee from the young man in bell-bottomed trousers (cut extraordinarily tight in the crotch), he got up from the velvet banquette, intent on getting down to using his initiative. 'You'll stay the night,' Lady Abney had said, and although he declined, protesting that he didn't even have a toothbrush and was in any case expected home, she finally forced him to stay at least to dinner. 'Now,' she said, 'you'll want to talk to Canning. I rather expect he'll be playing tennis with some of the other boys. Do you play?'

Bognor who, for one of his comparatively tender years, was grossly unfit, said, 'Yes, in principle'; to which she replied that next time he must bring his whites.

CHAPTER FOUR

The tennis court was shielded from the public by a very high brick wall, and as they approached it they could hear altercation. It was not clear what was prompting the argument but there was a general noise in which Bognor thought he could distinguish, occasionally, the words 'Yours', 'Mine', 'Shit', 'Christ', and 'Bloody hell'.

As they rounded the wall and emerged from the trees and shrubs which surrounded the court, the match was revealed in all its gladiatorial glory. All four men were extremely red, though it was hard to tell whether this was from physical exertion or bad temper. There appeared to be a lot of needle involved.

'I think,' said Lady Abney, leading the way to a wrought iron seat, 'that we had better wait until they've finished. They looked rather engrossed, don't you think?' Bognor agreed and they sat down to watch.

'The one with the bandana and the very short

shorts is Tony Grithbrice, Lord Arborfield's son,' said Lady Abney in a stage whisper.

'The photographer?' asked Bognor.

'Yes, and the one with the very long white trousers and the funny racket with the kink in it is Basil Lydeard. He's a poppet. And the handsome one with the silver hair is Canning. And the short one with the military manner and the moustache is Archie McCrum. He looks awfully cross, doesn't he?'

The McCrum, indeed, looked apoplectic. It was his service, and the previous interruption had clearly upset him even more than the others. He was having problems with it. Bognor watched as he took deliberate aim at Grithbrice who was standing in the opposite right-hand corner, and threw the ball immensely high. There was a mighty swish as he took a swipe at it, much too jerkily, and the ball shot over the net at a prodigious speed. Unfortunately the Scotsman was either too short for the game or had hit it at the wrong angle because the ball carried over the base line full pitch.

'Away,' said Grithbrice unnecessarily, and moved a couple of paces nearer the net. They all waited while the ball boy—one of four in blue shorts and gold shirts—retrieved the ball and lobbed it back to the McCrum, who was already engaged in bouncing his second on the ground preparatory to serving again. The lobbed ball confused him and he dropped both. Eventually

38

he retrieved one, glared at the ball boy, threw up the ball and very gently patted it at his opponent. It plopped softly into the middle of the net.

'Bother,' said the McCrum loudly. He had noticed the arrival of his hostess and obviously belonged to the school of thought which did not believe in swearing in front of ladies.

'Oh, bad luck,' said Grithbrice. 'That's game, I'm afraid.'

They moved to change ends and while all four took drinks from a silver tray at the side of the net Lady Abney called out to her husband to find out the score. It was a set each, and though the McCrum's dropped service represented a break-back for Grithbrice and Lydeard, they still trailed 3–5. It was Lydeard to serve.

It was already painfully obvious to Bognor that if Abney and Grithbrice were tennis players, the other two were not. It was not simply that Lydeard's efforts to serve were as embarrassing as McCrum's. It was the way they walked and held their rackets and wore their very old-fashioned outfits. Basil Lydeard began with a double fault to the McCrum and then managed a dolly drop to Abney who smashed it at an acute angle and with relish. Grithbrice made a brave effort to retrieve it and crashed into the netting.

'For Christ's sake,' he said, glaring at his

partner as he picked himself up. 'Have you played this game before?'

Lady Abney muttered something about it being very difficult to get ball boys these days and cupping her hands shouted out: 'Please, Tony, *pas devant les enfants!*' Basil Lydeard said, 'Sorry.'

Bognor, watching to see if the murderer was on court, wondered if the ineptitude of the two non-players was due to conscience or nerve failure, but as he watched Lydeard serve another dolly to the McCrum and saw *him* hit it off the wood and into a ball boy, he conceded that their failings had nothing to do with nerves.

'Where do the ball boys come from?' asked Bognor, as the boy rubbed his injured face. 'Some agency or other, I think,' said Lady Abney. 'We used to use the staff children, but it's become so devastatingly difficult to get proper staff nowadays that we've had to abandon that idea. Nowadays none of them seem to have children anyway.'

'Bother,' said the McCrum again, looking at the handle for an excuse.

'Try watching it on to the racket, Archie,' said Abney, fighting to appear casual.

'Basil Lydeard is such a gentleman,' whispered Lady Abney, whereupon the Marquis served another double fault. 'Fifteen forty,' said Abney. 'Match point.'

40

Lydeard turned to face Sir Canning, who sportingly hit the service over the base line with a gigantic lob. 'Thirty forty,' he said. 'But still match point. It's all up to you, Archie.' The McCrum said nothing, but to everyone's surprise the spirited off drive, which he aimed at Lydeard's next successful service, connected splendidly. The ball flew waist high at Grithbrice who attempted to avoid it but failed.

'Should have left that, Tony,' said Sir Canning, 'I think it was going out. Still. Game set and match. Hard luck, Basil. That wasn't at all a bad serve. It's always tough to be let down by your partner. Thank you, Archie.'

'I must try to play more often,' said Lydeard. 'It's really quite fun.'

'Not for the others, unfortunately,' said Grithbrice. 'How about singles, Canning? I'll play you the best of three.' Sir Canning looked at his watch. 'Better not,' he said. 'We've got tax in half an hour and Cosmo will be most put out if he doesn't get a packed house.'

There was, Bognor observed from his wrought-iron seat, a decided atmosphere. Abney and McCrum were not magnanimous winners, and Grithbrice had lost gracelessly. Only Lydeard seemed phlegmatic. He studied the four men.

Sir Canning, suave, well preserved with his silver hair and his manicured hands. He looked just a shade artificial, almost as if he was

41

wearing make-up and a foundation garment, but from a distance, or to the uncritical eye, the overall impression was certainly not counterfeit. He looked every inch a genuine eighteen-carat British baronet. Which, of course, he was. Bognor who had momentarily begun to suspect otherwise told himself not to be ridiculous; but still there was a petulance about the mouth which he found interesting and a little disturbing. Sir Canning was not a man he would lightly cross.

Grithbrice had the same sulky undertone, though at the moment his was more obvious since he was sulking. He was standing with his hands on his hips, watching Abney tip the ball boys, with a definite pout. Afterwards he put a powder-blue track suit top over his shirt and smiled in Lady Abney's direction, displaying rather more teeth than was necessary. There was no doubt that the man fancied himself, and Bognor conceded, with reason. According to the press he always had some glamorous female in tow, and he had lifted Netherly to third place in the stately home league without, apparently, compromising its traditional character. Nobody could explain how he had managed to attract four hundred thousand people a year without offending his father. Old Lord Arborfield, for years governor-general of Australia, was a crusty conservative figure, now confined permanently and pathetically to a wheelchair.

He was said to be mentally sound but those few who had attempted conversation with him recently came away with gloomy tales. Apparently he would talk about nothing but cricket, and then only in monologue, refusing interruption. It was therefore no secret that young Grithbrice was in control. Somehow he also managed to combine the running of Netherly and his adventurous sex life with a passable career as a photographer. Even Bognor, who believed that skill in photography was confined to the lab and the darkroom was forced to admit that he had taken some good pictures. That, however, didn't make him any the less conceited or obstinate.

He recognized both Lydeard and McCrum from photographs. Lydeard was older than he'd expected. The face was more marked with broken veins. It was a warrior's face though he seemed to remember that, in fact, Lydeard had failed to win a commission in the war and had been left to vegetate in Intelligence. Nevertheless he had a soldier's face. Something to do with heredity perhaps, because he came from a long line of generals which started with the Conqueror. He looked shaky from his exertions. Bognor wondered if he could have murdered Freddie Maidenhead. He could have poisoned him, he supposed, but hardly shot him. He looked too shaky for that, though it was true he had a remarkable and unwavering reputation as a bagger of grouse.

The last of the four was, Bognor knew, a real soldier, though his manner and his moustache almost suggested a catering corps parody. His real name, that is to say his English name, was Colonel Sir Archibald McCrum but he called himself the McCrum and the rest of the world followed. Every year his picture filled the papers when he presided at the annual gathering of the Clan McCrum at McCrum Castle, that massive gothic pile near Fort William which Bognor had once visited on a windswept day when it was too windy to climb the White Corries.

It was surprising his tennis wasn't better. Bognor watched him put his racket into its press with neat deft movements before straightening up and dabbing at his sweating forehead with a spotless white handkerchief. 'Thank you very much,' he said to the others, 'I enjoyed that.' It didn't look as if this was true but the others echoed him with ill grace.

'I could do with a swim,' said Sir Canning, then checked himself and blushed. 'Well, perhaps not today,' he said. As he left the court his wife pecked him peremptorily on both cheeks and introduced Simon. 'This,' she said, 'is Mr Bognor from ... er ... from Whitehall. He's come about George.'

Sir Canning looked rather mystified. 'About George? George who? Are you sure he hasn't

44

come about Freddie?'

'No, dear. He's come to arrange about George Mangolo and his visit and he's staying to dinner.'

'Oh, the Umdaka. Why on earth didn't you say?' Sir Canning looked greatly relieved. 'Oh well. First class.' He shook Bognor's hand. 'Good,' he said. 'Splendid. We'd better have a little chat. What would you like to know? I can't spare much time now, but later ... perhaps after dinner.'

'Well, actually,' said Bognor, as they walked slowly in the direction of the house, 'what I really want is a good chance to have a proper look round.'

'Oh quite,' said Abney. 'Why not spend a weekend? Bring your wife.'

'That's frightfully kind of you. I'm not married actually.'

'Oh well, bring a friend ... er ... I'd prefer female.' Abney looked faintly embarrassed. 'It just makes seating so much easier for the staff. I've no objection otherwise. Only we're two men up already with Cosmo Green and Peter Williams, so I'd prefer a girl if you don't mind.'

'That's fine, thank you very much.' Bognor wondered what Monica would make of it.

'Well.' They had reached the gravel forecourt. 'I'm afraid I really must go and change. Are you all right for now? Feel free to take a look round wherever you want and we'll see you at dinner.'

'There is just one thing,' said Bognor, 'about this morning. The um . . . er, accident.'

Sir Canning looked suspicious. 'I was afraid you might have come about Freddie,' he said, 'I'd rather you came out with it at once. I can't stand deceit.'

'No, I haven't come about Freddie,' Bognor found himself slipping too easily into the familiarity of first names. 'I mean, the Earl of Maidenhead. But his death is relevant to the Umdaka's visit. If it was the result of some security failure then we could hardly let the Umdaka come down here. At least not without laying on a lot of extra precautions.'

Sir Canning looked unconvinced. He scraped at the gravel with the handle of his racket. 'I suppose so,' he said. He was keen on the Umdaka's visit. It would give him some unsolicited column inches in the national papers. 'But Freddie's death is in very capable hands. The police are dealing with it.'

'Naturally,' said Bognor, who knew from bitter experience that it would be best to leave it to the police, 'but it *is* relevant. I'm sorry. I do realize it's distressing for everyone but it *has* happened.'

'Not distressing,' said Abney. 'A nuisance. Never mind. I suggest you have a word with Smith, the man in charge. All I ask is that you're discreet. I'm prepared to give you every help, even to the extent of having you here as my weekend guest, all I ask in return is your discretion. Can you promise that?'

'I'll try.'

'Good.' Sir Canning turned and went into the house, leaving Bognor to kill time until dinner. He decided to go and find Smith.

Smith was, after some initial sparring, extremely cooperative. More so than Bognor would have been if the roles had been reversed. He offered to show Bognor the corpse—an offer which Bognor, who was squeamish, declined. He showed him the bullet, from a .22 rifle, which had done the damage and he provided him with a complete list of guests and staff with his own thumbnail sketches to match. He also opined that the murder had been committed at about seven a.m. and that no one yet had a real alibi or a real motive, unless it was Peter Williams and Dora Maidenhead. Since they were clearly having an affair they might have a motive, though divorce would have been simpler. Since the police had already discovered that, far from breaking down in their boat, they had spent a comfortable and well-planned night together at the Compleat Angler in Marlow it looked as if they might have an alibi too.

In return for all this Bognor volunteered the information that the sights of one of the rifles in the miniature range were wrongly aligned. Smith said that the night before the murder all the men, Honeysuckle Johnson and Mabel McCrum had gone down to the range and done some shooting. The murder shot had almost certainly been fired by someone lying on the diving board to take aim. The range would have been less than twenty yards. Anyone with the slightest knowledge of how to work a .22 could have done it. By the time they'd checked the guns they all had fingerprints from several hundred members of the public on them. 'Including mine,' said Bognor wryly.

He also suggested discreetly that his department were concerned that the killing could have been politically motivated. Smith duly added the possibility to his list but was frankly incredulous. There were already, he said, the germs of sexual motives, financial motives, publicity motives, stately-home-jealousy motives as well as the possibility that there was no motive at all. However, if Mr Bognor wanted political motive to be investigated then naturally it would be investigated. The two men parted with mutual promises of cooperation.

Back at Abney, Bognor went for a stroll down by the river bank. The private gardens were shielded from the river by shrubs and hedging except at the area immediately around the diving board. It was odd that the Abneys hadn't built a pool, since the Thames was fairly filthy and swimming was a public matter which could only take place under public scrutiny. Perhaps that was why the board had been left. The chance of seeing near-naked nobles leaping into the river was a powerful additional incentive to Sir Canning's potential visitors.

Bognor stood for a moment by the board and then gingerly lay down on its length, drew an imaginary bead on the water about twenty yards away, then frivolously pulled an imaginary trigger and said, 'Bang, Frederick, Earl of Maidenhead, this is your death.' Immediately he regretted it, as a sultry voice from above and behind, said sarcastically, 'When you've finished your macabre little game perhaps you would allow me to use the board for its proper purpose?'

Bognor got up and dusted himself down. 'Miss Johnson, I suppose?' he said, putting out his hand. 'I'm Simon Bognor. We haven't met, but I've heard a great deal about you.' He realized as he prattled on inanely that she was staggeringly sexy. Her bikini, which was orange, set off her ebony skin to perfection. It was one of those miniscule garments in which the pieces appear to be connected with curtain rings. Bognor, who regarded himself as undersexed and who was in any case devoted to Monica, fancied her enormously. All this, he thought to himself, and murder too.

'Tony said there was some bum on the snoop,' she said crisply. 'You look like you

49

could do with some exercise. You're a very poor colour and a very bad shape. Now do you mind.' He moved to one side and she stared at him for a moment with only the mildest curiosity, then brushed past and dived swiftly and gracefully into the Thames. It was a shallow, almost a racing dive, and she came up to the surface almost immediately. For thirty yards she crawled, then changed abruptly to an immaculate, lunging butterfly. She reached Berkshire quickly and with no apparent effort. Once there she got out and stood, shading her eyes to peer back at the house. The lock at Cookham must have opened recently because a little fleet of assorted and nondescript pleasure steamers, cabin cruisers and launches churned past. From somewhere up in the public area a voice through a loud hailer urged the boats to slow down because of their wash. A few of the occupants waved and whistled at the nubile figure of Miss Johnson. She ignored them studiously and waded back into the now oily water before swimming lazily back. As she came to the board, Bognor knelt down and offered a hand up. She seemed to hesitate for a moment, then swam round to the steps at one side and clambered up unassisted.

'Could I ask you a few questions?' he said, diffidently.

'Gassy. Just gassy,' she said, towelling herself down in a manner which Bognor decided was

50

deliberately suggestive. 'I heard you were fixing up a trip for that old bastard Mangolo. So I don't see how I'm going to help there. And if you think I'm going to answer your creep questions like this, you'd better think again.'

'I'm awfully sorry,' said Bognor, reddening.

'Oh,' she said mimicking him, 'I'm awfully sorry too, old boy. But,' she dropped the imitation and came a step closer to Bognor, 'I'll tell you something for free. If you are interested in who did Fred this morning, just have a little friendly word with that faggot Cosmo Green.'

'Really?' said Bognor. 'Why?'

She came another step closer so that she was only a couple of feet away from him. She smelt of River Thames. 'Because, darling, he was in love with him. That's why.' Before he could demand an expansion of this unlikely news she had spun round and was walking back towards the house, her bottom wiggling in its inadequate orange casing.

'In love with him?' said Bognor out loud. 'Cosmo Green and Freddie Maidenhead? That's a bit steep.'

*   *   *

Dinner was at seven-thirty for eight. In the meantime Bognor had combed the grounds in a desultory sort of way not knowing quite what he was looking for, and had talked to the odd minion. No one seemed to come on duty before eight so no one admitted to knowing anything about Maidenhead's death. As for George Mangolo, Bognor was quite unable to find anything that looked remotely like a threat to his safety. He rang Parkinson, who sounded still irritable, and also Monica who was upset to hear that he'd be back late, but pleased at the idea of a weekend as the guest of Sir Canning Abney.

Drinks were served in the plum drawing-room. Drinks were champagne cocktails made with Dom Perignon and some very old brandy from Harveys. Bognor, who was a bit faddish about that sort of thing, thought this vulgar ostentation and a waste of both. However it was suitably anaesthetizing. As he entered the plum room he realized that he was out of place. Everyone else had changed. The ladies were in long dresses—even Honeysuckle Johnson who compensated for this formality by virtually dispensing with a top—and the men wore dinner jackets. Cosmo Green wore a maroon smoking jacket, Grithbrice a tobacco-brown suit with velvet reveres, and the McCrum a dress kilt with a huge dagger stuffed in his sock. Bognor thought there was some rule about not wearing the kilt south of the border, but he had to admit that the McCrum tartan looked less incongruous than the Bognor tweed.

'I am sorry,' he said to Lady Abney, 'I'm

afraid I wasn't able to change.' It was the suede shoes that were bothering him more than anything. The Spanish footman from whom he accepted his drink was looking at them witheringly.

'Don't be silly, dear boy,' said Lady Abney. 'You look perfectly splendid. I've put you next to Dora Maidenhead. She needs cheering up, so be nice to her.'

Bognor nodded.

'We'll have a word after dinner,' said Sir Canning, 'but come and meet my general manager, Peter Williams. He may be able to help.'

Peter Williams seemed tense. 'I can't see that there should be any problem with the Umdaka,' he said. 'We're fairly used to this sort of thing, you know. I mean, the fellow's only some well-connected aboriginal. We've done the real thing. Buck House and all that. I really wouldn't have thought there was any need for concern.'

Bognor was conciliatory. 'It's routine,' he said, 'that's all. The Umdaka isn't much liked in his own country and there are a number of Mangolan exiles over here who might try something on. It seems fairly far-fetched but we have to be sure.' He asked Williams a lot of routine questions and Williams gave him a lot of competent, reassuring answers about closed circuit TV scanners, burglar alarms and the vigilance and intelligence of the highly trained Abney staff. Bognor nodded throughout, but just before they went in to dinner he said: 'Still, after this morning, nothing is certain is it?'

'That's rather different,' said Williams, 'I mean first of all it was an inside job, and secondly it was a *crime passionel*. We can hardly guard against that, can we? It's just unfortunate he couldn't do it in the privacy of his own home.'

'Are you sure?' asked Bognor, intrigued.

'What?'

'Both. Inside job and *crime passionel*.'

'Oh I don't know. Forget I said it, I wasn't here so I don't know anything, do I? But that's what people are saying.'

'Ah. Yes, I gathered you weren't here. The boat broke down ... somewhere near the Compleat Angler, wasn't it?'

'I do hope,' said Williams looking apprehensive and cross, 'that there won't be any need to go into all that.'

'I hope not. It's not really for me to say.'

'How do you mean?'

'Well, there'll be an inquest. It'll be up to the coroner and the police. Not me.'

'But you are police.'

'Not really.'

At that moment Mercer came into the plum room and announced dinner. Everyone moved down the corridor in the direction of the private dining-room. 'This used to be open to the public,' said Sir Canning, who had evidently noticed that Williams and Bognor were not getting on, 'but I closed it a couple of years ago. After all they see the grand dining hall which is much more interesting. I really don't understand why they should see ours as well. And the smell in the evenings was indescribable. I'd no idea the public stank like that! Do you remember, Peter? We just couldn't get rid of that filthy B.O.'

'No,' said Williams. 'Even after we'd stopped them smoking it was still ghastly.'

'The last straw was when Isobel found a piece of used chewing-gum on her chair,' said Abney. 'I mean, I ask you, aren't people absolutely bloody?'

They had arrived by now in a well-proportioned oblong room, hung with heavy family portraits. Bognor had an impression of a great quantity of glass and silver worth a great deal of money but not of any particular beauty. He was sitting in the middle of one side of the table with Dora Maidenhead on his left and Cosmo Green on his right.

'I do hope you two boys don't mind being next to each other,' said Lady Abney, 'only we simply haven't enough girls. Never mind. Simon's bringing someone at the weekend so that will make things a little easier.'

Dinner was served by four girls in flowered

cotton overalls, watched over by the vigilant Mercer, and consisted of lobster bisque, grouse, syllabub and scotch woodcock. The grouse which was, of course, out of season, came from the deep-freeze. The Marquis of Lydeard was heard to observe that this was bad form.

There was sherry with the bisque, Château Talbot with the grouse, Château Climens with the syllabub and, later, a profusion of port, brandy, liqueurs and real Havana cigars which Grithbrice had procured from a friend in the Hungarian embassy. To begin with Bognor did his duty by Dora Maidenhead, who was not in the least downcast.

'So you're finding out what happened to Freddie?' she said, as soon as they'd sat down.

'No,' he said, 'I'm arranging a visit for the Umdaka of Mangolo.'

'You mean George.'

'I suppose so, yes.'

'He's divine. And terribly sexy. Five wives, my dear. Ten children and thirty bastards. I've always fancied him.'

Bognor was embarrassed.

'I'm not embarrassing you, am I?' said Dora Maidenhead.

'No. Of course not, not in the least.'

'Do you like sex?'

'Well, um, yes, I suppose, I mean it depends.'

'Depends on what? Do tell. I'm not

embarrassing you am I?'

Bognor looked round desperately, but everyone else was engrossed. 'No, of course not.'

'Oh dear, yes I am. To tell you the truth I've been drinking a bit. Not much. Just a little. I can't take it like I used to. I adore sex. Do you like drink? You look as if you do. Gosh, what have I said now? My dear, I am sorry. Anyway, who do you think did it? Have you any clues? It can't have been me or Peter Williams, we were having a dirty night out. Isn't it dreadful? It's not awfully nice to be out having sex when one's husband gets done in, is it? Not quite right, what do you think?'

'I really don't want to pry, Lady Maidenhead. And I'm honestly not investigating your husband's death.' He looked around again, even more desperately, and to his great relief, Basil Lydeard, who was on Lady Maidenhead's left, took up the challenge.

'First-rate soup, don't you think?' he heard him say, and turned away thankfully.

'You're the lucky man who owns Hook,' he said to Mr Green who was drinking his soup with an unpleasant slurping noise.

'Right,' said Mr Green. 'You been there?'

'Yes,' said Bognor, 'I particularly remember the Holbein in the hall.'

'Hook's a fine piece of property,' said Mr Green. 'Cost me five million pounds. Five

57

million pounds, did you know that?'

'No, I didn't. That's remarkable.'

'Wouldn't think I came from Latvia, would you?'

'No, I suppose not.'

'Well I don't, I come from Manchester.' Mr Green laughed immoderately. 'No, my old man, he came from Latvia. He had a little tailor's shop in Manchester. Pity he never lived to see his son dining with dukes. You got property?'

'A flat, in Regent's Park, actually.'

'You own it?'

'No, I rent it.'

'Silly boy, silly boy. You buy some property now before it's too late. Otherwise you'll never make money.'

'I rather like the flat actually. It's pretty.'

Mr Green looked at him sharply. 'You don't want to make money, is that it? That's what's wrong with the country. No drive. No initiative. Nobody wants to make money any longer. Even my good friend, Canning, he has to come to me for help. So did poor Freddie. What a shame. What a gentleman! Hey,' he leant forward conspiratorially, 'you want any help on this? Just ask me. Anything I can do. Here,' he reached in his pocket and brought out a visiting card. 'You take this. Anything I can do, you let me know. Anything at all, but especially about poor Freddie. I've got my ideas.' He tapped his nose, 'Not now, you understand. But you want this cleared up, then you come to me. I could tell you a thing or two. Good grief, yes.'

By now Bognor was feeling battered. He found some consolation in Honeysuckle Johnson's cleavage which faced him across the table, but she caught him staring, and he looked away again.

Somehow he got through the meal. With Mr Green he discussed lingerie and property and tax, the cornerstones, it appeared, of the Green fortune; and with Lady Maidenhead he discussed, incoherently, whether President Kennedy had been having an affair with Marilyn Monroe, whether Edward Heath had sex appeal, and whether Brighton or Le Touquet were suitable for dirty weekends. By the time the ladies retired he felt distinctly drunk. He also wanted to talk about something he understood.

For a few moments there was silence as everyone drew on their cigars. He looked round at the flushed faces. Everyone—Abney, Grithbrice, McCrum, Williams, Green, even old Lydeard, looked as if they were inebriated. Eventually, after everyone had had at least a sip and a puff, Grithbrice lay back in his chair and said languidly, and with a little slurring of the consonants:

'Well, gentlemen, the night is young. What entertainment shall we have now?'

'I don't know about you chaps,' said Basil Lydeard, 'but I'm pretty tuckered. I think I shall have a small nightcap and then take myself off for an early night.'

'Same goes for me,' said the McCrum, 'I'm just about ready to hit the palliasse.'

'Oh come on,' said Grithbrice, 'how about a game of "Johnny, Johnny"? Bognor, do you fancy a game of "Johnny, Johnny"?'

'Sorry,' said Bognor, disliking him increasingly, 'it's not a game I know and I'm afraid I have to drive back to London.'

'Oh, come. Canning, you'll back me. I'm sure the ladies will play. I'm damn sure Honey will anyway, and, Archie, I bet Mabel will have a bash.'

'I'll play,' said Williams, 'but I don't suppose half of us know the game. Will you explain or shall I?'

'O.K.,' said Grithbrice, 'I'll explain. Do I have your support, Canning?'

Sir Canning nodded. 'If you insist. Only not for long. I suggest a thirty-minute limit.'

'Done,' said Grithbrice. Once again Bognor was reminded of the petulance he'd noticed earlier on the tennis court. The man had to have his own way.

'It's a simple game,' said Grithbrice. 'Full name, "Johnny, Johnny, strike a light." We draw lots to see who'll be Johnny. Then we all go outside and count to a hundred while Johnny

60

goes and hides. When we get to a hundred we call out, "Johnny, Johnny, strike a light," and "Johnny" strikes a light from the box of matches with which he is provided. He flings it in the air and everyone sets off in pursuit. It's really a sort of "He" only in the dark. It has all sorts of possibilities.' He grinned. 'It usually ends up sinister or sexy. Everyone on?'

Nobody but Williams, Grithbrice and to a lesser extent Canning, seemed keen but they all appeared to think a refusal to play would involve loss of face. A muted approval was gained and Grithbrice went off to tell the ladies. Five minutes later he came back, happy.

'They agree on one condition, that there are no "Joanna's". In other words only the men are hunted. That seems in keeping with the contemporary role of the sexes, so I agreed on your behalf. So. Let's drink up and begin. After all, Mr Bognor has to get back to London and Archie and Basil have to get to bed.'

Outside it was very dark. There were clouds and a stiff breeze so that although some stars could be seen, the moon was behind cloud most of the time. Every so often it emerged for a few seconds and the outlines of the trees and of the house were clearly visible. Grithbrice had got some matches in his hand. 'Everyone draw one,' he said, 'and the one who gets the used one is Johnny.'

They drew the matches in silence. 'Well?'

said Grithbrice. 'Mine's not used.' There was a chorus of 'Nor's mine,' and then the McCrum said, 'It looks like me.'

'Do be careful, Archie,' said Mabel McCrum, 'look out for the river.'

'O.K.,' said Grithbrice, 'off you go.'

The McCrum, kilt swirling in the breeze, trotted stiffly into the dark towards the cedar tree, and the rest of them began to chant out loud. 'One ... two ... three ...' Bognor shivered. It was chill, and the wind whipping off the river in the direction of the house made it damp too. This was, as far as he was concerned, a bloody silly way to spend an evening. 'Fifty ... fifty-one ... fifty-two.' The moon came out for a second, throwing the branches of the trees into sharp relief. 'Eighty-one ... eighty-two ... hurry, Archie, we're coming soon.' Bognor looked round at the rest of the party. Not one had thought to put on any extra clothes. The ladies were going to freeze. Especially the Johnson girl. Already she was clasping her arms to her largely naked bosom. 'Ninety-eight ... ninety-nine ... one hundred.'

'Now,' shouted Grithbrice. 'All together now. Johnny, Johnny, strike a light.' The chorus echoed across the river and faded into the noise of the wind in spring leaves. They waited in silence for the McCrum to strike a light. 'Hope he hasn't dropped them in the

62

river,' said Dora Maidenhead, just as, away in the direction of the tennis court there was a sudden tiny light which arced up into the blackness and equally suddenly fizzled out.

'O.K., everyone. Fan out and charge!' shrieked Grithbrice, who became more enthusiastic by the second. Sir Canning's dinner party obligingly disappeared in the gloom. Bognor, who had no wish to play a leading part in the proceedings, which he already found embarrassing, started at a run towards the court, but when he reckoned he was out of sight, slowed to a walk and ambled towards the cedar in the direction of the river. He decided to hide underneath it and wait for the charade to finish. He had been standing, leaning against the trunk for the best part of a minute, shivering slightly, when he thought he heard someone coming towards him. Looking round he could see nothing in the pitch black. All the same he could swear there was someone close. He was about to call out, when the person leapt at him, pinned him to the cedar and began to kiss him passionately on the mouth. There must be some mistake, he thought, struggling to free himself. He tried to speak, but any attempt was frustrated by increasingly passionate and professional kissing. After a few seconds Bognor began to enjoy himself, but who on earth could it be? It smelt very feminine and rather alcoholic. He prayed to God it wasn't

Cosmo Green, or even Sir Canning. But no, he had a strong impression of female breasts. Whoever it was, was strong and very determined and experienced.

'Got him,' came a cry from about a hundred yards away. It sounded like the insufferable Grithbrice. 'Got him. He's tripped over the net. Help!' As quickly as she had begun, Bognor's mystery lady disengaged and vanished into the night.

For a moment Bognor stayed exactly where he was, spreadeagled against the trunk of the cedar and panting slightly. Then he took out a handkerchief and felt his mouth. It was quite sore. What an extraordinary thing. Nothing like that had ever happened to him before. A case of mistaken identity, he supposed. He was almost certain it had been female, which narrowed it down to four. If it had been the Johnson girl then it had obviously been mistaken identity, and anyway he had an idea his assailant had been older. Mabel McCrum was out of the question. She was too short. So it must have been Lady Maidenhead or Lady Abney. Rather embarrassing either way. Still, he had to admit that after the initial surprise it had been rather fun. He hoped, though, that it had been a mistake and that there would be no follow-up. That could be very difficult. Particularly if Monica or Parkinson were to find out. He wondered if he should tell Monica.

As he mused in this perplexed way he was walking slowly back towards the house. Just as he passed a large rhododendron he was once again conscious of a person close to him, and once again he was not quick enough in taking evasive action. A hand spread over his mouth and an arm tightened round his throat.

'Just stay right away from Tony,' said Honeysuckle Johnson. ''Cos if you get nosey, you'll get very hurt. Just remember. Stay away.' Then without warning, she too disentangled herself, and made off into the darkness. Again Bognor was breathless. 'Oh bugger,' he said out loud and straightened his tie. This was getting silly.

Back at the garden door he found that he was the last to arrive back. Everyone, including Miss Johnson, seemed perfectly composed, except for the McCrum who was hopping about and massaging his ankle. 'Bloody silly place to have a rope,' he was saying. 'Could have killed myself.' But no one paid much attention, not even his wife.

'Come along, Bognor,' said Grithbrice. 'We want to do another. Hurry up.' He held out matches once more and the men all picked, except for Archie McCrum who said he'd had enough of being Johnny. This time it was Grithbrice who got the used match. 'I warn you, I shan't be so easy,' he said, jogging out of sight. Sir Canning started the count. Bognor

65

looked at the Ladies Maidenhead and Abney. Dora Maidenhead looked tipsy. Isobel Abney sober and unruffled. Perhaps it had been one of the maids. Maybe Sir Canning employed a nymphomaniac staff to minister to his guests' needs.

They reached a hundred when the moon was behind cloud, and the wind had risen a little so that it was difficult to hear, 'Johnny, Johnny, strike a light,' they shouted lustily and watched. A second later Bognor, who had been gazing absent-mindedly at the sky saw a match flare about sixty feet up. 'There,' he exclaimed. 'Up there. In the cedar.'

'You're right,' said Abney. 'He's climbed the cedar. Silly fellow. Still he'll be down it by the time we get there. And incidentally I don't advise anyone else trying to go up it. Not even you, Peter, it's too dangerous.'

They set off again, less eagerly this time. Bognor wondered if the mystery kisser would strike again and, to his shame, rather hoped she would. Provided he didn't know who it was it didn't matter. He decided to walk down to the side of the river and see what happened. He was there about five minutes, vaguely conscious that there was a lot of running about. Once two figures sprinted across the lawn ten yards from where he stood and another time he heard a crash and some heavy swearing. Nothing else. He strolled along the bank until he was next to the diving board and stood there staring at the river, which was choppy now, with tiny little white horses just visible even without moon. He felt a drop of rain and shivered. It was getting absurdly inclement. Again he heard the sound of running and two men passed him again, one chasing the other. He could make out their shapes dimly but it was impossible to see who they were. Then there was more swearing away to his left. It sounded like frustration, as if the hunter had lost his quarry. Then the footsteps—only one pair this time, came back in his direction, slowly at first—then faster. They were coming, he realized with the wakening of alarm, straight at him. Oh, God, he thought another mistake. It was too. The footsteps were closing fast. Too late he tried to get out of the way, but before he could step aside he felt two hands in the small of his back, heard an anonymous voice whisper, 'Drown, you little sod,' and realized with horror that he was being pushed towards the river. He was only feet from the bank and his shove backwards to safety was too little and too late. He staggered forward, tripped on the top of the steps, and took a mouthful of oily, freezing water as he pitched into the Thames, head first.

CHAPTER FIVE

His first attempt at a shout for help came out as a strangulated gargle. He floundered wildly for a second and tried to touch bottom with his feet. Too deep. Still, even in a tweed suit and with suede shoes he was a passable swimmer and he was only a couple of yards from the bank. He trod water for a moment, spitting and retching and shivering and then struck for the shore. He made it in two strokes, grabbed hold of the bottom rung and started to pull himself up. As he climbed he saw that his attacker was standing at the top of the ladder, though he could only distinguish a dim shape.

'Give us a hand,' he said, putting one hand up towards the bank. 'Don't just stand there.'

Suddenly the man moved. Before Bognor could move his hand, he brought his right foot down on the fingers hard and then aimed a kick at Bognor's head which caught him a glancing blow above the left ear. Bognor fell back into the river with a sharp cry of pain. The cold water revived him. There was no point in trying to climb back again. The man was a maniac. He'd never make it. He trod water a few feet out and shouted, 'Help! Man overboard. Help! Can't swim.' It was bitterly cold and the current was strong. He did a couple of strokes upstream to prevent himself following the Earl of Maidenhead down to Cookham Weir and bellowed again.

'Help! For God's sake, someone. Help!' His left hand was quite numb and his head hurt where the man's shoe had caught it. He took another mouthful of Thames and gasped. This wasn't in the least funny. 'Help!' he shouted again, when to his relief there was a sudden flash and the whole of the river bank, the house, the cedar, the grounds and even the guests were illuminated.

'There he is,' he heard someone shout. 'There, down by the diving board.' He swam back to the steps. With the floodlights on he was surely safe. They couldn't all be trying to murder him. He started to climb again. It was agony with his injured hand, but Sir Canning was kneeling solicitously at the top of the ladder and hauled him up.

'Good God, man,' he exclaimed. 'You must be frozen. Mercer. Get blankets and brandy. Hurry.' The rest of the guests looked on in apparent disbelief and then started to chatter inanely among themselves. Bognor was too dazed and numb to say anything. He just stood and shivered while Mercer and a maid draped blankets round him and gave him brandy.

'Find him some dry clothes,' said Sir Canning. 'And get him dried out.' He turned to Bognor. 'How are you feeling now, old boy?'

Bognor's teeth chattered and he nodded vagely. 'That's all right, don't try to say anything.' Sir Canning looked at him with what was evidently intended to be a clinical expression, and said, 'I don't think we need worry about a doctor. Mercer and Lucy here will get you fitted out in some dry things. You'll be all right after a few more glasses of that.' Then he turned back to his other guests. 'Come on, the rest of you,' he said, 'I think we could probably all do with a drink.'

Quarter of an hour later Bognor was wearing a pair of brown brogues, two sizes too big for him, a pair of spongebag trousers which were a little too tight round the waist and were consequently kept in place with a very frayed old MCC tie, an olive-green silk shirt from Turnbull and Asser, an Old Etonian square (to which he was not entitled) and a blazer from Gieves which was too wide on the shoulders. Mercer had made a nourishing hot drink for everyone which was based on warm brandy and egg yolks and the entire party was sitting in the library where a log fire was burning. Two salukis and an Italian greyhound, which Bognor had not met before, were stretched out in front of the grate and the voice of Oscar Brown emanated from the stereo outlets at each corner of the room.

'Must have tripped,' said Bognor, who was still sober enough to be careful what he said.

'But couldn't you get out?' asked Grithbrice. 'I mean you can swim. After all it's eight foot, even under the bank there, and you must have been in for at least five minutes.'

'I must have panicked,' said Bognor, 'and it was too dark to find the steps. Besides I bruised my hand when I fell.'

'That's a perfectly horrid cut on your temple,' said Isobel Abney, looking concerned. 'How on earth did you manage to do that *and* bruise your hand? Poor lamb, you do seem to have been dreadfully clumsy.'

'Anyway,' said Sir Canning, 'it's hardly a very friendly welcome to Abney and I can only say that I am extremely sorry. Of course, you'll stay the night.' Bognor wondered if the nymphomaniac maid would be provided.

'No,' he said, 'I really would like to get back.'

'Only on one condition,' said Sir Canning, 'and that is that you won't drive yourself. I don't think you're in any state to do that.'

'Oh really, I'm fine. Honestly.' He had to admit, however, that he didn't feel fine.

Sir Canning moved over to a bookcase and pressed a button. The middle two shelves moved to one side, revealing an internal telephone. He dialled a number and then said: 'Perkins. Have the Rolls outside in ten minutes would you ... London ... No, Mr Bognor ... Hang on.' He turned to Simon, confirmed the

71

address and told Perkins it would be Regent's Park.

★   ★   ★

Half an hour later Monica sat up in bed, yawned, rubbed her eyes, and said: 'Good God. Have you looked at yourself in a mirror?'

'No.'

'You look terrible.'

'I feel terrible.'

'You'd better have a drink.'

'I've had a drink.'

She looked at him more closely. She was properly awake now.

'Yes, you have, haven't you? And you've fallen over. And why in God's name are you wearing those ludicrous garments?'

'It's a long story.'

'Well,' she sighed. 'Even if you don't want a drink, I do.'

She got up and went out of the bedroom in search of scotch.

'I'll have one too,' he called after her. She was wearing a sexy nightie, but he had to admit that compared with Honeysuckle Johnson she was on the plain side. Still, he was fond of her. At least he supposed he was; it was a long time since he'd bothered to think about it.

She came back with the glasses and gave him a kiss.

72

'Hey,' she said. 'That's really nasty. Do you want a plaster?'

'It'll be all right.'

'Well take those things off and get into bed and tell me all about it.'

He did as he was told. Eventually, when he'd told her everything, including the sexual assault, she sighed a long long sigh and said: 'And after all that you're honestly going back to spend the weekend, *and* expecting me to go with you.'

'Yes.'

'But next time they may make a better job of you.'

'It was a mistake.'

'Like the kiss?'

'Like the kiss.'

'Huh.'

'Huh what?'

'People don't make mistakes like that.'

'They do in the dark.'

'Even less in the dark.'

'Anyway you don't have to come.'

'Oh, I'll come. If you're going to be bumped off by some loony in a stately home I'd rather be around to see it. How are we getting there?'

'The Rolls is coming at eleven. I think I'm going to make a list. Have you got a pencil?' Bognor always made lists when under severe stress or when totally perplexed. It helped hm to arrange his mind.

'You are not, repeat *not* making a list. Not now. In the morning. If you want to know who did it, it was the McCrum.'

'He couldn't. He'd hurt his ankle.'

'Subterfuge. Anyway I don't mean the river I mean the kiss. Much more important.'

'Do you love me?'

'Mmmm.'

'Prove it.'

⋆   ⋆   ⋆

Next morning Bognor was struggling with his list and some scrambled egg when the phone rang. 'It's for you,' said Monica, 'Basil Lydeard.'

'Basil Lydeard?'

'Yes.'

Monica had her hand over the receiver. 'Help,' he said, 'how do you address a Marquis on the phone?'

'Your Grace?'

He took the phone from her. 'Good morning, your ... er, good morning, it's Simon Bognor here. Can I help you?'

'I found your name in the phone book,' said Lydeard. 'Not a very usual name. Any relation of Sir Humphrey?'

'Distant.'

'Ah. Old chum of mine. Give him my regards when you see him.'

74

'Of course.'

'I'm in a phone box.'

'Oh!'

'I'm not ringing from Abney. Slipped out for a moment. So we can talk freely.'

'Good.'

'Yes. Well not to beat about the bush, I have a nasty feeling you didn't fall last night. My hunch is you were pushed.'

'Whatever makes you think that?'

'I could be wrong, I suppose, but I think I have an idea who might have done it. Without wishing to tell tales, of course.'

'Of course not.'

'Just before it happened I was being chased by Grithbrice.'

'Chased by Grithbrice? But we were supposed to be chasing him.'

'I know that, only as you probably noticed the fellow was getting fearfully over excited. Anyway I gave him the slip, and then I think he made off towards the river, and pushed you in.'

'But why should he do a thing like that? And why should he chase you in the first place?'

'He knew I was on to them.'

'Sorry?'

'On to them. Him and the girl. All this Mangolan nonsense.'

'I'm terribly sorry,' said Bognor. 'This is an awfully bad line. Could you speak up?'

'Mangolo,' shouted Lydeard. 'Brother of

mine was governor there. Recognized that Johnson girl straight away. Bad lot those Johnsons. Smell them a mile off.'

'Are you trying to tell me that Honeysuckle Johnson comes from Mangolo?'

'Course. Must go now. Talk to you later. Someone coming.'

There was a click and the line went dead.

'Funny,' said Bognor, 'Lydeard says the Johnson girl comes from Mangolo.'

'That follows,' said Monica.

'Why?'

'I don't know. Intuition maybe. She just sounds a bit too good to be true.' The phone rang.

'That'll be him again,' he said, 'he had to hang up in a hurry. Hello,' he said into the phone. 'Bognor speaking.'

There was the rapid 'pip ... pip ... pip' of a call box then his caller put the money in.

'Hello, Bognor? It's Tony Grithbrice here.'

'Oh. Good morning.'

'Look, I think I may owe you some sort of an apology for last night?'

'Oh?'

'Well, I have a suspicion you didn't fall into the river.'

'Go on.'

'Am I right?'

'Um ... ?' Bognor decided to stall. This was becoming confused. He had hoped Grithbrice was going to confess. 'Tell me more.'

'It's just a feeling I have, and Honey agrees. I think whoever did it was trying to get me.'

'What makes you think that?'

'I can't swim.'

'Can't swim?'

'No.'

'You realize what you're saying.'

'That someone wanted to kill me?'

'Yes.'

'Yes.'

Bognor sucked his teeth, another nervous tick which affected him, like list-making, in moments of stress or perplexity.

'How many people knew you couldn't swim?'

'Oh, everyone. It's a standing joke. There's no secret about it.'

'So who would want to kill you?'

'Anyone you care to mention.'

'Why?'

'I'm not exactly popular but there are a number of specific reasons. I'll tell you later. Anyway I just thought I'd let you know.'

'It's very kind of you. I might add that if someone did push me in the river it might perfectly easily have been you.'

'No motive.'

'Because I was asking too many questions about the Umdaka.'

'So?'

'Well, your girl friend comes from Mangolo,

doesn't she?'

There was a pause and then he said tersely, 'I suppose that interfering old bugger Lydeard told you that. He was in the phone box when I got here. I thought he looked shifty. I'll have to talk to him.' They were interrupted by more pips as the call box ran out of money. 'No more change,' said Grithbrice, 'I'll talk to you later when you arrive.'

'Funny,' said Bognor, putting the phone down. 'Suddenly everyone wants to tell me things. I wonder why?'

'It must be your frank open face and your winning boyish ways,' said Monica. 'More coffee?'

Bognor said yes and went back to the list. From the zoo he could hear indeterminate animal noises. They reminded him of his stately peers. One of them was a murderer. Worse, he appeared to be on the verge of striking again. He pencilled in 'Political motive' against Johnson's and Grithbrice's names and sucked the pencil.

In the left-hand column of his list he had written down the name of each of Sir Canning's guests as well as the Abneys themselves. Every one of them could have killed Maidenhead, except his wife Dora and Peter Williams, who were at the Compleat Angler. On the other hand it would have been no great problem for one of them—or both—to leave the hotel, go to

Abney, shoot Maidenhead, and get back without being spotted. But risky. Grithbrice and his girl friend might have done it in the cause of African nationalism but that was far-fetched.

Sexual jealousy? Had Maidenhead really spent the night with Cosmo Green? Was there some business or financial motive? Green could help with that too. He remembered the little man tapping his nose at dinner the night before and felt in his pocket for the card. 'Cosmo Green,' it said, 'Hook, Herefordshire, Telephone Number, Hook One.'

'I think,' he said to Monica, 'we'll try to engineer a drink with Cosmo Green, before we actually get to Abney. I'll get the Rolls to drop us off at the Feathers.'

      ★   ★   ★

An hour and a half later Monica and Bognor sat in the saloon bar of the Feathers, waiting for Cosmo Green. He had expressed himself delighted to be able to help, quite understood the need for discretion and had agreed to meet them in the pub at eleven-forty-five. Bognor ordered two gin and tonics and the two of them eavesdropped as the barman chatted to the only other occupant of the bar, a clergyman with a Welsh accent.

'Big do down at the boat museum today,' said

the barman.

'So I hear,' said the cleric, who was drinking Guinness. 'Mind, I don't know it shows proper respect for the dead. And him not yet buried.'

'Shocking business.'

'Terrible.'

'They do say,' here the clergyman leant forward and they had to strain to hear, 'they do say there's a lot of carrying on. That Lady Maidenhead, for instance. Not a great example of marital fidelity, or so I believe.'

'Come to that,' the barman was also talking very conspiratorially, 'they say old Freddie wasn't above a bit of hanky-panky. Got himself a bit of Scotch crumpet, I heard.'

For a giddy moment Bognor wondered if they were talking about Mabel McCrum, but the clergyman was disputing it. 'I'd always understood he was keener on men than women myself,' he said, 'though I shouldn't say it really, him being only just dead.'

'What Sid Grubb at the boatyard always used to say was "No member of either sex is safe with the Earl of Maidenhead in the back of a taxi,"' said the barman. 'Not that he ever had to take a taxi.'

Unfortunately this revealing conversation was halted by the entrance of Cosmo Green, who was wearing white flannel trousers, a yachting blazer with anchors on the brass buttons, and a beige turtle neck shirt.

'Simon, my boy,' he said, removing the immense dark glasses, which had been shielding his eyes and accentuating his nose, 'I'm sorry to have kept you. And this must be Monica. Delighted to meet you, my dear, and what can I get you? Would a Pimms be nice? Three Pimms, if you please, barman, and a pint of what you fancy for yourself, and make one of the Pimms without a cherry if you wouldn't mind.' He indicated his stomach. 'Have to watch the figure at my age, you know.' He sat down and patted Simon on the knee. 'Terrible business about last night. Terrible business. Whatever happened? You know if I didn't think I was being silly I'd think you were pushed in the river. If you want to know what I think, I'm afraid we haven't finished with all these unpleasant things.'

The Pimms came and they all said 'Cheers'.

'What can I do for you, then?' asked Mr Green.

'Well,' said Bognor, nervously. 'For a start I wonder if you could tell us how well you knew the Earl of Maidenhead.'

'Freddie?' said Mr Green, shaking his head and smacking his lips. 'Like a brother.'

'Through business?'

'Through business to start with of course, but later on we were just buddies. Like I said, he was like a brother to me.'

'I don't want to seem personal, Mr Green,

81

but . . .'

'Personal, personal, you go ahead, you be as personal as you like, and call me Cosmo. All my friends call me Cosmo.'

'Well, did he owe you money?'

'Sure he owed me money. They all owe me money. Sir Canning, he owes me money, the Grithbrice kid, he owes me money. Even old McCrum, he owes me money. Only person who doesn't owe me money's Lydeard. Would never lend him a farthing. Not a farthing. And for why? Because his security's so terrible. Nothing to secure it with. Terrible.'

'Did Maidenhead owe you a lot of money?'

'Not as much as he did. A few thousand, that's all.'

'Really?'

'Simon, I'd like to help you, but I can't give numbers.'

'Oh all right.' Simon took a swig of Pimms. 'Was your friendship with Maidenhead, well, was it anything more than a friendship? I mean.' He went rather red. 'I mean was it any more than . . .'

'What Simon is trying to say,' said Monica, 'is "Was your relationship with the Earl of Maidenhead homosexual?"'

Bognor shut his eyes and counted to ten, but Mr Green was unabashed. 'Me and Freddie Maidenhead?' he said, smiling. 'You must be joking. Freddie and Mabel McCrum maybe.

Me and Freddie, no. He was too much of a gentleman for that. Besides,' he lowered his voice still further below the extreme sotto in which the conversation had so far been conducted, 'that sort of thing never works when there's money involved.'

There was a pause while they all drank more Pimms and avoided looking at each other. Then Mr Green spoke again:

'Tell you what, though. One or two things you don't know. They may help you a bit. Abney and Grithbrice aim to merge, soon as Grithbrice's old man passes over. "Abney-Arborfield Enterprises." Joint publicity campaigns, joint ticket sales. Be a big business. Should do well, specially Stateside.'

'Who would that threaten?'

'Could threaten everyone.'

'How would it have affected Maidenhead?'

'Not too good. They tried to get him to come in on it.'

'Oh?'

'He didn't play. Said he was big enough already.'

'So that's another motive?'

'Another motive?' asked Mr Green. 'You have one already?'

'Sort of,' said Bognor. 'What else can you tell us? Was Maidenhead really having it off with Mabel McCrum?'

Mr Green looked shifty. 'Maybe I shouldn't

have said anything about that,' he said. 'There's no proof. So. You know we have a proverb in Yiddish which says, "A fool is his own informer." Shall we go?'

They drove on to Abney in Mr Green's emerald green Aston Martin (numberplate CG 1), and on the drive Mr Green used the car telephone to say they were coming.

'I'm awfully sorry,' said Bognor to Lady Abney when they arrived. 'But I wanted to have a quiet word with Mr Green about business. I hope you don't mind.' Lady Abney gave his hand an extra squeeze, and was studiously polite to Monica. He wondered if it had been her the night before. She didn't look strong enough.

Their room looked out over the Thames and across the National Trust land opposite, to Winter Hill. It was lavishly furnished with a fourposter bed, a fridge full of drink, a bottle of Balenciaga scent on the dressing table, and two John Pipers and a Helen Bradley on the walls. Bognor left Monica to unpack, and sauntered downstairs in the hope of finding someone else interesting to talk to. He had forgotten until the pub conversation that the grand opening was that afternoon, but it was not until four p.m. Because of it, there was a definite air of 'business' and there was no one about until he wandered into the library and found Basil Lydeard, immersed in *Sporting Life*.

84

'Ah,' said the Marquis, 'I was having a gin. Have a gin.' He rang a bell and a Spanish servant appeared. 'Pink gin for Mr Bognor,' he said, 'and another for me. And a bit more gin this time, if you don't mind.' He waited until the man had left before saying, 'Damn foreign servants. Won't have them myself.'

'That must make life difficult.'

'We manage. Get a very good class of servant in our part of Somerset. None of your home counties' nonsense.'

'No. By the way, thank you for telephoning.'

'Telephoning?' He looked muddled, and then brightened. 'Of course. Yes.' The Spanish servant came back with the gins, which were large and almost neat.

'Yes,' continued Lydeard, when the man had gone. 'Thought I ought to let you know. Wouldn't do to have them hanging round the place when George Mangolo turns up. Could lead to no end of trouble.'

'Yes.' Bognor coughed on his gin. 'Are you quite certain this Johnson girl comes from the same family as the ones you remember?'

'Certain. Rang my brother Hubert to check. This one's the worst of the lot. She'll hang if they get her back. Deservedly too. Professional agitator of the worst sort.'

It seemed to Bognor that for a man with such an enviable reputation for charity and peacefulness Basil Lydeard was being unusually bloody and thundery. 'I'll have to look into it,' he said.

'You won't get much chance today,' said the Marquis morosely. 'All these shenanigans over Canning's steamboats. Place'll be full of journalists.' He pronounced the word 'jawnalist', and with contempt. 'Rather have foreign staff than journalists.' He sighed. 'I don't know,' he said. 'Sometimes I think I'm getting a bit old for all this larking about with the bison. Never thought about having bison until Bath imported all those circus animals. Sometimes I think it might have been better to sell up. Still there's been a Lydeard at Lydeard since 1143 and I'm not budging, even if it means bison.'

'Why did you open in the first place?'

'Death duties, same as everybody else. Not that it makes much difference. Never made money out of opening. Lost a whole herd of bison during foot and mouth. Set me back a small fortune.'

'Good heavens. How did you replace them?'

'Sold a Canaletto.'

'Oh.' It was a difficult remark to follow.

The two of them were staring self-consciously into space, wondering what to say next when the door opened, and four strangers entered. It was immediately clear, both to Bognor and Basil Lydeard, that not only were they strangers in the sense that they had not been introduced

86

but in the sense that they were aliens. Interlopers, no less. They comprised a family: a father of middle age with receding hair, heavy National Health spectacles, baggy grey flannel trousers, a windcheater and a pair of those heavy leather sandals which looked surgical but aren't; a wife in tight, bulging tartan slacks, and a cardigan over a loud check shirt; an adolescent son kitted out much like his father; and a slightly younger daughter in a cotton printed dress. Father carried a camera, the two adults also had guide books and all four were chewing. On entering the library they betrayed no sign of embarrassment or guilt, no awareness of trespass. Instead they closed the door behind them and stood alternately consulting the guide books and peering about the room in the general direction of Bognor and Lydeard.

''Ere, Mavis,' said Father, tugging at his wife's sleeve, 'look at this. Must be worth a fortune.' He pointed at a huge and particularly ugly plate salver which Bognor had noticed the previous night. It had been presented to the Abneys at their wedding by the tenants on the surviving Abney lands. (Most had almost immediately been dispossessed. Perhaps, thought Bognor, in retribution for so foul a wedding present.)

'Solid silver, that is,' said Father, 'and over a hundred years old by the look of it.'

Bognor, not wishing to cause any

confrontation, slid a hand surreptitiously in the direction of the morning's *Daily Telegraph* on a nearby table, intending to hide behind it. Even perhaps to derive some harmless entertainment from the family's comments. However he was spotted.

'Hey, Dad,' said the boy, in a loud whisper, 'look at that. One of them moved.'

'Shhhh. Your mum and I are looking at something.' The two continued to stare, misty-eyed, at the salver. They had evidently spotted the inscription, and were reading it to themselves. Their lips moved in unison and after a moment Mavis touched her husband's elbow. 'That's lovely,' she said. 'That's really lovely.'

''Ere. Mum, Dad.' The daughter had also, apparently, discovered that the two men at the other end were alive. 'Do you think we ought to be in here?'

The two parents looked at her with irritation. 'What you talking about, Else?' asked her mother peevishly. 'Just have a look at all those wonderful books.' She moved over to a bookcase and screwed up her eyes to read the titles. '*Power to Destroy*,' she enunciated carefully. '*A study of the British tax system* . . . *Portnoy's Complaint* . . . *Tropic of Cancer* . . . *The Female Eunuch* . . . *Mysteries of Orgasm*.' She paused. 'Fred,' she said, 'look. I think these are dirty books.'

'Don't be soft,' said Fred. 'Look at that picture. That's nice.'

'Don't care for that sort of thing myself,' said Mavis sniffily. It was a Hockney. Bognor hadn't cared for it either.

'Mum, Dad, will you listen?' The two children had woken to the true situation rather more quickly than their parents. Bognor, embattled behind the *Telegraph*, looked round the corner of the paper at Basil Lydeard and was alarmed to see that he had gone a dangerous shade of scarlet.

At the other end of the room the family of interlopers were in conference. It was strained. Bognor heard:

'You been nothing but a nuisance ever since we left Croydon.'

'I tell you, it's private. Where do you think everyone else is, if it's not private.'

'I paid my bloody money. Course it's not private. Nothing's private. It's open to the public, innit? Open. O-P-E-N.'

'Fred. Language. It's not nice.'

'Dad, we're not supposed to be here. Look at that man, the way he's watching us.'

'Let him bleeding watch. Who is he anyway?'

'It's probably him.'

'What, him?'

'Yes, Sir Abney.'

'So what if it bleeding is? It's a free country.'

'Dad!'

89

'Fred!'

Bognor heard a sudden movement from the armchair on his left. Lydeard could evidently stand it no longer. Expecting him to beat a dignified retreat and find another haven somewhere else in the house, Bognor settled down to the paper. He was surprised a second later to hear that the Marquis was not leaving. Instead he was joining battle.

'Now just look here,' he heard him say, with only a trace of his usual querulous diffidence. '*This* is a scandal. Now get out immediately, before I throw you out.'

Not for the first time that morning, Bognor shut his eyes and counted to ten.

'Now just *you* look here, mate,' he heard Fred say. 'I don't know who you are, but we paid our money to come in here and look at some of these priceless pieces of heritage and we're not leaving till we seen them.'

Bognor peered round the *Telegraph* and saw, to his horror, that Lydeard was wielding a poker.

'You'll be out of here by the time I count ten, you horrid little oik, or you'll be prosecuted for trespass. *One, two* . . .'

'I paid my bloody money, you bloody old man, and I'll bloody stay until I want.'

'*Three, four* . . .'

'Oh, come on, Fred, let's get out, I don't think he's right in the head.'

'I'm frightened, Mum.'

'*Five, six* . . .'

Bognor, who didn't like the way Lydeard was waving the poker, decided that it was time to intervene, coughed loudly and stood up. 'I say, er . . . Basil,' he began, but was saved from more decisive action by the door, which opened, revealing Monica.

'Good heavens,' she said, taking in the scene, and then spotting Bognor, she smiled. 'Oh, good. I thought I'd find you in here.'

Bognor moved to the door. 'Hello,' he said, 'Monica darling, this is the Marquis of Lydeard. Basil, this is my fiancée, Monica.'

'Ah, How do you do,' the Marquis put out a hand and then realizing that it contained a poker withdrew it again. Then he dropped the poker noisily and re-extended the hand. 'How do you do.'

'How do you do,' said Monica, 'I'm sorry, I hope I wasn't interrupting anything.'

'No, no, that's quite all right.' Lydeard's complexion had reverted to its usual mottled purple and he seemed to have regained his composure. 'No, I'm afraid I became a little over-excited by some trespassers.'

'Well, they've gone now, anyway,' said Bognor, going to the door and peering down the corridor. He could see the retreating rears of the interlopers at the far end, heading back into the public sector, muttering. He closed the door. 'One of the inevitable hazards of being in this sort of business, I suppose,' he said lightly.

Lydeard glowered and then relaxed. 'Shouldn't happen in a well-run household. Never happened at Lydeard. Had to see off a couple of journalists once, but that's rather different.' He turned to Monica. 'Have a gin?'

Monica nodded and said yes, and the old man rang the bell. After a few minutes of relatively idle chatter the room started to fill in readiness for lunch. Lydeard had asked if Bognor would mind very much saying nothing about the incident. 'No point in embarrassing Abney,' he said. 'He's got a trying day ahead of him.'

The only person who could be embarrassed, was, of course, Lydeard himself, but Bognor agreed. It was a trivial matter, best forgotten. Instead the two men found common ground in a tribute to some giants of Somerset's cricketing past, and Lydeard's humour was much restored with a description of a cricket week he had once organized forty years earlier when a team, captained by him, had defeated the Somerset Stragglers, the Devon Dumplings and a strong I Zingari XI. In this welter of unlikely reminiscence, the interlopers were put out of mind. Bognor only hoped they wouldn't make some formal complaint and ask for their money back.

In view of the afternoon's excitement lunch was, by Abney standards, a hurried unceremonial affair. Conversation centred exclusively on the new steam exhibits and was of a flattering sort. Lydeard, suffering perhaps from guilt, even asked if he could have a private preview of the *Lysander*. A request which was greeted with approving acquiescence. Honeysuckle Johnson was conspicuously silent throughout, but all the others were, between mouthfuls of caviar and salmon trout, garrulously ingratiating. Sir Canning was particularly impressive, discoursing with equal eloquence on the significance of the voyage of the *Charlotte Dundas*, the possibility of planning permission for the inevitable new car park, loaded governors and double-beat lift valves, the China Mutual Steam Navigation Company, the possibility of acquiring a proper maritime site for bigger and more spectacular vessels and Gooch's link motion.

Afterwards Monica and Bognor went for a stroll.

'You've never called me "your fiancée" before,' she said. 'Absolute cheek!'

'It seemed appropriate. I don't think Lydeard would approve of "girl friend", not without a chaperone.'

'You could be right. What exactly was he doing with that poker?'

Bognor told her.

'He's a bit peppery, isn't he?' she said, when he'd finished.

'Liver, I should think.'

'But he wouldn't have shot the Earl just because he was having trouble with his liver?'

'Hardly. But anything's possible here.'

'Who do you really think did it?'

'Could have been anyone, couldn't it?' They sat down on the lawn near the cedar, and Bognor took out a diary and started to make another list.

'Ready?' he said, pencil poised. 'Right, Men first. Abney could have killed him because he wouldn't merge the business. As Dora's having an affair with Peter Williams, Abney might think she would be more malleable without a husband.'

'If you ask me she'll be having an affair with you next.'

'That's silly. I suppose he did leave the estate to her? I know there isn't supposed to be a direct heir, but there could be some forgotten cousin in Australia.'

'Doubt it.'

'Williams next. Motive. He wanted Dora and he'd rather like the estate too.'

'But he has an alibi.'

'Almost. Of course he and Abney might have plotted it together. Next one, Grithbrice. He has the same business motive as Abney. He wanted the merger just as much. Then he has a political motive, at second-hand anyway.'

'Through Miss Johnson? She looked a sulky

bitch at lunch.'

'But sexy?'

'Not particularly. Just black and busty.'

'That's rather what I meant.'

'Well, he'd hardly murder for her. Anyway I don't see why, just because she is a leading Mangolan nationalist, she should want to murder the Earl of Maidenhead?'

'He might have negotiated a settlement with the Rhodesians. That would be bad news for any African nationalist, so he'd be better dead.'

Monica sniffed. 'I think you'll have to do better than that.'

'That's what Smith said. The trouble with people outside the department is they always think things are simple. They never are. They're always incredibly complicated. I think we'll find the whole thing is an elaborate plot with everyone implicated and with a number of interlocking motives. Lydeard's liver, coupled with a general wish to expand the stately home industry into Rhodesia under the Abney-Arborfield banner.'

'That doesn't take Mr Green into account.'

'No. He has two motives. I bet he was having an affair with Maidenhead. Perhaps they had a tiff. Then again, he owed him money, and I'll bet it was more than just a few thousand.'

'All right. Two motives for Mr Green. That leaves the McCrum.'

'Sexual again. Maidenhead was having it off

with Lady McCrum.'

'You surely don't believe that?'

'Why not?'

'She's a podgy little suet pudding.'

'Probaby very good in bed.'

'I should think the McCrum would be glad to have her off his hands. What's her name, the McCrumba?'

'Mabel.'

'Well, there you are, then.'

'Where?'

'The Earl of Maidenhead would never have an affair with someone called Mabel.'

'He married someone called Dora.'

'Oh, all right.' She pouted. 'What about the women?'

'I don't think it was a woman.'

'Why not?'

'Because I think the person who pushed me in the river was the same person who murdered Freddie Maidenhead, and I was pushed in the river by a man. I saw his legs when I was trying to climb out.'

'That's speculation.'

'So's everything,' said Bognor gloomily. 'Well, women then, if you insist. The Johnson girl we've discussed. We can mark her down in the book for political.' He did so. 'Dora Maidenhead because she wanted to be free to carry on with Williams. I think that's unlikely. First of all she was very happy being Lady

Maidenhead, I'm sure. Second she was at the Compleat Angler that night, and thirdly she'd never have shot him. She'd have put something in his tea or stabbed him with a pair of scissors.'

Monica sighed. 'Why scissors? You're so typical of a man. It would be very clever to shoot him because all men would automatically assume that it had been done by a man. Shooting is a male crime. Men shoot people. Women stab people with scissors. If I was a man and wanted to do the perfect murder I'd use scissors. Everyone would assume automatically that it has been done by a woman.'

'I still think Dora's unlikely.'

''Cos she kissed you.'

'That leaves Mabel McCrum. She'd hardly shoot him if they were having an affair.'

'Male chauvinist,' said Monica. 'You're at it again. If Cosmo Green could kill him because they had a tiff then so could the McCrumba.'

'I wish you wouldn't call her the McCrumba.'

'Well, couldn't she?'

'Yes, if you insist,' he said testily. 'So absolutely every single rotten person had a motive.'

'You've left someone out.'

'No. Who?'

'Lady Abney.'

'Gosh. So I have. I'd forgotten about her. Does she have a motive?'

They thought. Monica was picking daisies. Bognor sucked the end of the pencil and watched the moorhens' heads jerk. 'You know,' he said, at length, 'I don't think she has a motive.'

'Just at the moment she may not,' said Monica, 'but she will.'

Bognor was on the point of upbraiding her for this cynicism when, with much theatrical coughing, Grithbrice and Miss Johnson came marching towards them hand in hand.

'Sorry,' said Grithbrice. 'We're not interrupting are we?'

'Not at all,' said Bognor. The two newcomers sat down beside them.

'What are you going to recommend about the Umdaka?' asked Grithbrice, his semi-Afro haircut waving in the breeze. Bognor look hard at the sensitive, aristocratic face, and wondered.

'I think,' he said, 'I should be able to recommend that he come here and look at the boats. Subject to one or two conditions.'

'Like, I suppose, that we're not here,' said Honeysuckle Johnson, coolly.

'Well, yes, actually,' Bognor tried to look at her evenly, but found her sexuality disturbing, 'I mean, if, as I understand you are a leading member of the Mangolan nationalist organization or whatever, I can hardly agree to let you within range of the Umdaka.'

'Do you realize,' asked Grithbrice, 'that that

tyrannical old bastard has actually had two members of Honey's family burnt alive? Do you have any conception of what he's done to that country?'

'Look, I'm awfully sorry,' said Bognor, 'I'm not a politician. I have to do as I'm told that's all.'

'Huh,' Miss Johnson smiled. 'Look, all I want is to get to talk to him, that's all. Just talk. I don't even know if my father and mother are alive out there.'

'They disappeared after the revolution,' said Grithbrice, 'or what our papers referred to as "the abortive coup". Nobody knows if they were killed or if the Umdaka locked them up.'

'I'm sorry,' said Bognor, 'I really am, but you must see my position.'

'Like hell,' said Miss Johnson.

'Oh, be fair, Honey,' said Grithbrice, 'he's only doing a job.'

'That's what I object to. How in God's name can you do a job without any conception of the moral issues involved?'

'That's not fair,' said Monica, 'Simon has a perfectly good idea of the moral issues involved; and you're not making it any easier for him.'

The two women glared at one another.

'Why don't you ask Sir Canning to intercede with the Umdaka?' asked Bognor.

'He never would. First he's a sight too impressed with the Umdaka's noble lineage and all that crap about the Umdakadom going back two thousand years; and second, despite his liberal mouthings he's pretty near as fascist as Archie McCrum when it comes down to it.'

'You don't sound exactly well disposed towards your future business partner.'

Grithbrice was startled. 'You're brighter than you look, aren't you?' he said, crossly. 'I wonder who told you that. Can't have been Lydeard this time, he doesn't know. Anyway, nothing's signed or agreed except in principle. I'm not at all sure it would work. It sounds great in theory, but it could just mean more paperwork.'

'I understand you tried to get Lord Maidenhead in on the act.'

'Not me, that was Canning's idea. Freddie was too flash for my liking. But what exactly are you getting at?'

'Nothing. It's nothing to do with me.'

'You're right, I don't think it is.' He got up and brushed down his trousers. 'Well, I just thought I ought to put you in the picture. There's nothing secret about it though. We're starting an Anglo-Mangolan Friendship Society soon, and it'll be announced in the normal way. There's nothing to hide. Come on, Honey, we'd better go and change for the great event.'

'Well, well,' said Bognor. 'What do you make of that?' He and Monica watched as the young Anglo-Mangolan friends lolloped back to the house. As they neared it they were passed by Mercer on his way out. He held a tray in front of him and was advancing in the direction of the cedar.

'Disingenuous,' said Monica, sniffing. '*She's* awful, but he's quite sexy in an effete sort of way. Look, butler ahoy! I think he's coming for us.'

Mercer was indeed coming for them. On arrival he held out the tray, and said, without expression, 'Telegram, sir, and Sir Canning's compliments, and could you please take your seats by three-forty-five?'

'Thanks.' Bognor took the small yellow envelope. 'Oh, Mercer, is Mr Smith about today?'

'Mr Smith of the police, sir?' Bognor wished he wouldn't make the 'sir' sound so derogatory.

'Yes.'

'No, sir. I should imagine that Mr Smith takes the weekends off. Will that be all?'

'Yes, thank you.' After he'd done, he said to Monica, 'Do you think he has a motive? He's terribly suspicious, and he doesn't care for me.'

Monica told him not to be sensitive. 'What's the telegram?'

He read it out loud. 'Understand Mangolan girl terrorist Abney guest. Take seriously. Report soonest. Parkinson.' Bognor smiled. 'Good,' he said, 'for almost the first time in my life I do believe that Parkinson is a step behind.'

101

CHAPTER SIX

Opening the steam section on a Saturday afternoon had been a calculated risk. Because it was a ticket-only affair it meant barring the general public on a day which would normally have been lucrative. Nevertheless Sir Canning's public relations consultants, Intercommuniplan, had suggested that it was worth aiming for the Sunday papers, and with the retainer he paid them, Sir Canning could hardly afford to ignore their advice.

Now, of course, the demise of Freddie Maidenhead had so whetted the appetite of the popular, and indeed the unpopular, press that there was no problem in attracting journalists. Unfortunately they were going to be more interested in the scene of the crime than any promotional activities. Already there had been inquiries of a sort which Sir Canning actually found irritating but which for reasons of tact he affected to find distressing. He batted them all back to Intercommuniplan who had eventually telephoned him to suggest that the only way to prevent further unpleasantness was to hold a press conference and, as Mr Eric de Villiers of Intercommuniplan put it, 'get the whole thing out of the way'. Accordingly a gathering of crime reporters was arranged to take place at two-thirty in the boardroom. On the advice of Mr de Villiers a large quantity of beer and whisky was provided.

Bognor who sat in at the back of the room found the appearance of the crime reporters as uncongenial as did Sir Canning. They were, for the most part, purple-faced individuals with baggy trousers, stained waistcoats and indifferent breath. Sir Canning, who was in shirtsleeves to indicate informality and industry, seemed almost effiminate by comparison.

Mr de Villiers, short, sleek and heavily scented, supervised the drinks and set the conference in motion. 'Gentlemen,' he said, in sepulchral tones, 'all of you are naturally aware of the sad reason for this meeting. Sir Canning, as you know, was a close personal friend of the late Earl, and he is very concerned that the very natural public interest in his death should be satisfied as soon as possible. Naturally there will be an inquest and therefore there are certain areas where obviously we shall all have to tread very carefully. However, Sir Canning and I thought it best to ask you here first before this afternoon's festivities where of course this sort of discussion would be er ... inappropriate.' He smiled unctuously and sat down.

Sir Canning was obviously going to be businesslike. 'Thank you all for coming,' he said, 'I think it best if we move straight to questions.'

There was an immediate babble of interrogation. Sir Canning looked desperately at Mr de Villiers who, with some presence of mind, said quickly, 'Gentleman at the back in the check overcoat.'

The person so designated identified himself as the representative of one of the more lurid Sunday papers and said, 'Who do you think did it?'

'I'm afraid I really can't comment.'

'Off the record, then.'

'Not even off the record.'

Another journalist interrupted. A smoother, more plausible person.

'Would you say there was much rivalry between the Earl and other stately home owners?'

'A little, yes.'

Questions continued. Sir Canning said less and less more and more verbosely and the press became restive. After twenty minutes a silver-haired reporter with a gold watch chain asked: 'May I put it to you, Sir Canning, that the only reason you asked us here is to avoid any difficulties and embarrassment later on this afternoon when you open your new museum?'

Mr de Villiers leapt to his feet. 'I really think that at a time like this,' he said, 'that's a most improper . . .'

'I wasn't asking you,' said the man in the

gold watch chain.

Sir Canning smiled diffidently. 'Naturally,' he said, 'we're all very concerned to get this whole thing settled once and for all and out of the way. Equally I really don't think we want to have any gloomy nonsense at this afternoon's party. I'm absolutely certain that that is what Freddie would have wanted. As he himself would have said, "the show must go on". And now, gentlemen, if you'll excuse me . . .'

There was much muttering and discontent but the press finished their drinks and left. It had not, Bognor reflected, been altogether satisfactory.

*   *   *

Notices had been placed in the press to warn the public that the house would be shut from two p.m. but even so the local police were busy turning visitors away at the gates. Inside, a small temporary grandstand had been erected on the river bank, at an angle which allowed the 250 guests to see both the harbour and the Thames itself. The guests were a mélange of nautical folk, round-the-world yachtsmen, admirals, newspaper proprietors, politicians, laced with starlets, film actors, and television personalities. Most of the male faces were recognizable and the majority of the female figures predictable. The invitation stipulated

'Edwardian dress' and a number of men had taken this to mean gaily striped blazers, flannels and boaters. Women—Monica included—seemed to have conducted a raid on Laura Ashley and were nearly all wearing long white lacy dresses, with flecks of red and purple on aprons and sashes and blouses. A few women—mainly the models and the starlets—wore as little as possible, usually in the form of very short shorts, with a sleeveless top, or tight trousers with bare midriff. Bognor had found an old pair of cricket trousers and a school blazer. He had also discovered his Upper Sixth boater at the back of a cupboard but he refused to wear it, on the perfectly accurate grounds that it made him look ridiculous.

At three-forty-five the guests had stopped milling about the banks of the river and the harbour and were settling into their places. Despite the breeze, the sun shone warm. A Royal Marine band played selections from *HMS Pinafore* and *The Pirates of Penzance*, and a profusion of bunting fluttered gaily from every available post, pole and piece of rigging. The Abney house-guests had a privileged place near the centre of the middle row of the stand, from where they had an unimpeded view of the small floating platform, with microphones, alongside which the *Lysander* was moored, already getting up a head of steam.

Bognor surveyed the scene with quiet

satisfaction. The air of subdued carnival was agreeable, and he had quite forgotten the deceased Earl of Maidenhead and the impending Umdaka. So, it seemed, had everyone else. Reds and yellows and blues and greens and silvers and whites proliferated, but not an inch of mourning black could be seen except behind the red rope a few yards to the right of the stand, where the gentlemen of the press sat cordoned away from the rest of the world in black and dark grey suits which sagged at the elbows and knees.

There were television cameras and still photographers; usherettes in blue and gold cat-suits with satin sashes, and in the background a festive marquee for the champagne tea. Bognor consulted his glossy programme. It appeared that first of all there would be speeches from the platform, from Sir Canning, then from the captain of the *Queen Ann*, who had a reputation for plain and amusing speaking. (He was supposed to be a friend of Prince Philip.) Then the two men alone would embark on the *Lysander*, leaving the normal crew behind with the captain's lady and Lady Abney. The steam pinnace would sail out of the little harbour, do a very quick turn down the Thames, while the captain and Sir Canning acknowledged the plaudits of the crowd and the band played 'Rule Britannia' and other appropriate airs, and while, most important of all, the cameras rolled, the photographers snapped and the gentlemen of the press dutifully scribbled away in their shorthand notebooks. The boat would then go about, re-enter the harbour and moor once again by the floating platform. At this point the exhibition would be technically declared open by the captain, and guests would be free to follow the official party as they toured round gawping, on their way to the drink tent.

Bognor glanced along the line of guests. The Abneys were still in the house, doubtless having a tot of grog with the guest of honour, and Peter Williams could be seen in the distance organizing away in blazer and white trousers which had razor-sharp creases. Otherwise everyone was present. Not one looked in the least bereaved or the least guilty. Bognor was inclined to think the whole thing was a bad dream.

A few minutes before four there was a ripple of applause and the four principals came walking towards the gang-plank which led to the floating platform. Lady Abney and the captain (whose name was McAvity) led, followed by Sir Canning and Mrs McAvity. Isobel Abney looked striking in an unusual gold trouser suit, heavily flared and tied at the waist with an electric-blue silk sash. Captain McAvity wore what Bognor presumed was the dress uniform of a merchant navy captain. It looked like an old-fashioned station master's, consisting simply of dark blue serge and an excessive splattering of scrambled egg. His wife was neat and just the safe side of dowdy in a navy blue suit and matching hat. Sir Canning himself would no doubt, have brought a blush to the cheeks of his Victorian forbear.

To Bognor his appearance, which had changed radically since the press conference, suggested a number of images, all wildly inappropriate. They were, roughly: Naples, co-respondents, ice-cream, and amateur theatrical productions of *The Boy Friend*. The outfit which prompted these thoughts consisted of brown and white spotted shoes, cream-coloured Oxford bags, yellow blazer with a blue stripe, the Abney arms (presumably) on his breast pocket, and a pale blue cravat secured with a pearl pin. The finishing touches were, arguably, the most bizarre. On his head he wore a dinky little yachting cap, of the pillbox sort favoured by Scandinavian students on graduation days; and under his left arm he carried a brass telescope.

'My God,' said Bognor to Monica, 'what does he look like?'

'Failed gigolo in Italian operetta on a bad day at Glyndebourne,' she said. 'No, correction. Pinkerton in a school production of *Madame Butterfly*.' Sir Canning's appearance seemed to have much the same effect on the rest of the audience, but luckily the band's spirited rendering of 'A Life on the Ocean Wave' drowned the resulting titter although Bognor distinctly heard the McCrum mutter, 'Fellow looks an out-and-out pouf,' and thought he heard Mabel McCrum tell him not to be so 'rude and vulgar'.

With a final flourish the band stopped and Sir Canning took to the microphone. It was not an inspired speech. 'Great privilege to have with us Captain McAvity ... ran away to sea as a boy ... sailed round Horn ... immense changes in modern seafaring ... highly skilled ... greatly honoured to have him open an exhibition of which very proud ... fine complement to existing display ... inevitable step forward ... many years of devoted work by team of dedicated experts ... pay tribute to tireless work and understanding of wife ... of Peter Williams ...' Bognor's attention wandered to the showpiece, moored alongside the speaker. It was a beautiful boat, though he was completely ignorant of such things. She was, he supposed, about forty feet long and very low in the water. The bows back to the long thin brass funnel which rose absolutely vertically amidships, were decked in highly-polished pale wood; but behind the funnel there was an open cockpit where two men could be seen crouched, presumably over the boiler. Behind the funnel there was a large wheel and a small dashboard

110

of knobs and dials. From the stern a gold and blue triangular pennant fluttered. Unless people were to stand on the deck there was scarcely room for more than two people. He wondered what the Grand Duke Leopold had wanted it for. Showing off, probably, which was, after all, the same reason as Sir Canning's. A polite round of applause woke him from his day-dreaming. The first speech was over and it was now Captain McAvity's turn. Captain McAvity's turn was a characteristically bluff and salty one, well honed by repetition at twenty-five guineas a time. He invariably salted it up a bit for businessmen's luncheons and down a bit for ladies' literary guilds, but he gauged this audience as 'genteel and bisexual' which meant that he cut out the one about the Englishman, the Scotsman, the Irishman and the Welshman in a Venezuelan brothel but left in the one about the Pope's visit to Paris.

'Three cardinal rules, stand up, speak up, shut up ... great pleasure and privilege to be here ... reminds me of occasion on which Pope visited Paris ... he said ... she said ... so he said ... so she said ... Well I feel a bit like that ... immense industry and vision of Sir Canning ... made Britain famous for this sort of thing ... as Nelson said to Lady Hamilton ... whereupon she replied ... absolutely certain of immense success ... extraordinary omen when funny thing happened on my way here ... she

111

said to me . . . I said to her . . . so she said to me . . . May I say once more . . . very great privilege . . . my wife and I . . . heartfelt thanks and appreciation . . . warmest wishes for every deserved success.'

Bognor who again drifted off after the opening sentences was sure he had heard it before but was prepared to admit that it was such a production-line effort that he could have heard it from someone else, although, equally, it was so boring that he might have forgotten it. Eventually the captain sat down and Sir Canning returned to the microphone.

'Ladies and gentlemen,' he said, 'I hope you will bear with me just a little more. All I want to say is that Captain McAvity and I are now going to take a short . . . and I mean short . . . trip in this magnificent steam pinnace which you see in front of you and which was specially commissioned by the Grand Duke Leopold almost a hundred years ago. For the purposes of posterity and history we have decided not to officially open the exhibition with any cutting of red tape or smashing of bottles. Instead as we return upstream we shall simply give one small blast on the *Lysander*'s whistle and at that moment the steam section of the Abney small ships museum will be open. Ladies and gentlemen, thank you once again for coming today, I hope very much to see you in a few minutes' time with a glass of champagne in the marquee.'

The band now struck up with more Gilbert and Sullivan, and Captain McAvity and Sir Canning began to embark. The two looked hardly ready for any real voyage, no matter how short, Bognor was struck once again by the absurdity of Abney's outfit and reflected that even the captain looked unreal, like a Madame Tussaud's sailor. He glanced across at the choppy water of the Thames and hoped they wouldn't disgrace themselves by being riversick.

'Hope they don't capsize,' giggled Monica. 'It doesn't look frightfully safe.'

The professional experts, the two men who had earlier been huddled in the *Lysander*'s cockpit, were now giving Abney and McAvity, some final instructions. From the bewildered demeanour of both of them it looked as if they were more first than last minute instructions. The senior of the two men was gesticulating, making pulling and pushing and winding movements and shaking his head vigorously. Sir Canning was nodding unimpressively, like a small boy taking delivery of his first paddle boat in the park. Eventually the embarkation was complete, the crew cast off, the band struck up with 'Rule Britannia' and Sir Canning, standing precariously behind the wheel, steered the boat out into the river with one hand, while waving with the other, Captain McAvity, standing

113

beside him with nothing to do, looked distinctly uneasy.

Despite the peculiar appearance of its two passengers the boat had class. Its sleek lines and shiny fittings demonstrated for everyone, the good taste of the Grand Duke Leopold and the expertise of the vessel's designer. Nevertheless as they hit the Thames and turned left down river (Bognor had never had any truck with such terms as port and starboard) there was a nasty moment. The wind in midstream was stronger than in harbour and obviously stronger than Sir Canning had realized. He swung the *Lysander* too sharply and for a moment as she lurched dangerously and several waves broke over her deck, it seemed that the worst might happen and she would indeed capsize. The issue hung in the balance for a second and then she righted herself and started to push down the Thames towards Cookham and out of sight, with clouds of smoke belching from the funnel.

'She does look rather like a sea-going bonfire,' said Monica.

'Hardly sea-going,' said Bognor.

'Nice for picnics, though.'

'I suppose.'

'I'd rather have a punt.' She touched his arm. 'We ought to do that some time.'

Similar conversation began all around as the band changed to Handel's *Water Music*, performed in crisp military manner, doubtless reserving the rest of 'Rule Britannia' for the *Lysander*'s return. Although the boat was out of sight of the VIP guests on the Buckinghamshire bank, quite a crowd of hoi polloi had built up on the towpath on the Berkshire side, which being owned by the National Trust was, of course, open to them. Some had obviously gone there by design to observe the festivities but others were simply afternoon picnickers and dog walkers. The progress of the boat could be followed from the grandstand by the loud and enthusiastic cheering of this multitude, the younger of whom ran along the towpath keeping alongside the boat. The gentlemen of the press, meanwhile, had broken out from behind their barricade. Some swarmed along the Abney bank snapping off film, while the older among them had already disappeared in the direction of the drink tent, and a very few intrepid ones had put to river in a small motor boat. Eventually the hubbub announced the impending return of the *Lysander*. A light pall of smoke lay in a swathe several hundred yards along the river, the band returned to 'Rule Britannia' with great verve and at last the bows of the boat returned to view, making slow progress against wind and current.

As the vessel, with its two captains now looking distinctly ruffled, came opposite the narrow harbour mouth, she seemed to slow, ready to turn in. At this point it was generally agreed—later it was almost the only thing that was generally agreed—she was almost exactly in midstream, that is to say some thirty-five to forty yards from either bank. Abney and McAvity had been busy waving, saluting and generally gesticulating in the direction of both lots of spectators. But as she slowed both men stopped this and, it seemed to Bognor, suddenly became alarmed. Abney began to raise an arm and although Bognor was not so sure, it was later agreed by most that this was to sound the inaugural whistle. But the whistle never came. Instead there was a sudden blinding flash and a mighty explosion, followed almost immediately by pandemonium. Men and women began to scream. Some clutched their faces from which blood poured freely, the band of the Royal Marines, after faltering briefly, continued to play 'Rule Britannia'; a posse of tipsy journalists came rushing from the drink tent and ran headlong into an advance party of fleeing starlets and TV personalities, a voice on megaphone (later found to be Peter Williams) exhorted people to stay still and not panic, and in the middle of the river, where the *Lysander* had been, there was a dense and dreadful cloud of steam and smoke and a gentle, sinister, hissing noise.

'Jesus Christ,' said Bognor, immobilized by shock. He looked round to Monica. 'You all right?' he said shakily. She was very white but apparently unhurt. 'Is everyone all right?' he asked more loudly, and inanely, and looked along the row of Abney house guests.

They all looked very pale and several had been cut by flying debris of some sort. Mabel McCrum was clutching her arm and moaning. Her husband, blood flowing from a cut in his neck was wrapping a large spotted handkerchief round it and shouting: 'It's only a bloody scald, woman.' Basil Lydeard, apparently unhurt, was sitting motionless with tears streaming down both cheeks. Grithbrice whose girl friend was bleeding from her head and shoulders, but who appeared quite composed, was jumping about shrieking, 'Doctor! Doctor, for Christ's sake someone get a doctor!' Cosmo Green could be seen struggling down the stairs holding his hand to his right eye and Dora Maidenhead was sitting in her place laughing hysterically. Bognor told Monica to try to shut her up, and decided to move down to the centre of things to see if he could help. In the distance he could hear sirens starting, and already after barely seconds, some sort of order was being imposed. Two or three doctors had come forward and the band, which had now stopped playing, were acting as medical orderlies. The drink tent had become a field dressing station, and it seemed from a first questioning that most people's injuries were superficial. 'Cuts, scalding, shock,' said a busy professional-looking man who was tying lengths of torn shirt round wounds. 'But *they* hadn't a hope, poor buggers.'

For whatever reason—fear, futility, simple selfishness—no one except the photographers was paying any attention to the mess in the middle of the river. Bognor hurried to the water's edge and peered through the smoke and steam which still lay heavy on the surface. He was joined a moment later by Peter Williams.

'Pointless, I'm afraid,' he said flatly, staring into the fog.

'I suppose so,' said Bognor. Then a thought struck him, belatedly. 'What about Lady Abney and the captain's wife?'

'Taken care of,' said Williams gloomily. 'I've sent them off with Dr and Mrs Nolan. They're friends, which helps. I imagine he'll put them both under sedation.'

'How were they?'

He shrugged. 'How would you be?'

'Don't you think we ought to do something?'

'Yes, but what?' Williams half turned to look at the subsiding confusion behind him. The sound of fire appliances and ambulances and police cars indicated imminent arrival. 'I don't think anyone is badly hurt,' he said, 'and the organization's here now.' He smiled bitterly. 'You forget, we have a highly-trained staff to deal with big occasions.'

'But surely,' said Bognor, 'we ought to go and have a look at . . .' his voice trailed away, 'at the *Lysander*?'

'I hope,' said Williams, sounding near breaking point, 'there'd be nothing to see. But I'd rather not find out if you don't mind.'

Nevertheless they continued to peer into the fog. It was beginning to drift away slightly now and they could see a big oily patch of water spreading slowly towards the banks and downstream. Tiny pieces of wood and fabric showed up on the surface but nothing remotely recognizable. Bognor moved to the very edge and leaned over. There among reeds and undergrowth was a blue and white object with something gleaming in the middle of it. He lay down on the bank and put an arm down to reach it. It was firmly lodged between two boughs, but he pulled it free after a couple of tugs, and stood to examine it. It was the dinky pillbox yachting cap he had been so scornful of a few minutes earlier. He stood holding it at arms' length, wondering what to do with it, and feeling terribly guilty.

'I'll have that if you don't mind.' Bognor turned and recognized Smith, the policeman.

'Of course,' he said, and handed it over. 'I'm glad to see you,' he said fatuously, but meaning it all the same.

'I'd like a word in a minute or two,' said Smith. 'Don't go away.' Bognor sat down feeling deflated. Peter Williams went off to be busy. Bognor recognized the therapeutic nature

119

of the mission, and watched Smith organize the cordoning-off of the bank. Over on the other side of the Thames, now visible again, he could see uniformed police conducting a similar exercise. He wondered if the drink was being served, and was just thinking he might sneak over to see, when Smith returned carrying a champagne bottle and one glass. 'It may seem inappropriate,' he said, 'but you look as if you could use a drink and everyone else is hard at it in the tent. You'd think they'd all go home wouldn't you? I'll never understand about people.'

Smith managed to open the bottle without an ostentatious pop and Bognor gulped at it. It was very cold and dry. Under any other circumstances he would have appreciated it, but at the moment he would have preferred brandy. He was feeling distinctly queasy.

'What a ghastly accident,' he said, choking slightly on the drink and then retching.

'Accident?' said Smith.

'Presumably. That old tub was almost a hundred years old. It can't have been safe and quite honestly I don't think Sir Canning knew how to work it.'

'Well,' Smith looked suspiciously at the dirty water. 'I wonder if we'll ever know.'

'How do you mean?'

'We'll have to put down divers, but I don't imagine they'll come up with anything very conclusive. I don't suppose there was a black box flight recorder on board.' He laughed harshly. 'I don't somehow think they're going to find an awful lot of Sir Canning Abney and Captain James McAvity either.'

Bognor retched again, and Smith looked at him unsympathetically. 'Except that we have his hat,' he added.

'I don't think that's particularly funny,' said Bognor, wondering if Monica had managed to calm down Dora Maidenhead, and if so, what she was doing now. He felt like some moral support against this callousness.

Smith looked at him again, hard. 'You really think it was an accident?'

'I don't know. How should I know?'

'You're the clever one from Whitehall.'

'I'm not a trained detective, I'm a civil servant. Of sorts.'

'Pull the other one. You're not as silly as you make out or I'm a virgin.'

'Honestly, at the moment I have no ideas at all.'

'Look,' said Smith, 'I know you've had a nasty surprise, but the rest of us have had a nasty surprise too, so be a good boy and give me some bloody help because right now I need it, frankly. I'm going to have my Chief Constable going bloody spare over this. So please.'

'What do you want to know?'

'Anything.'

'Well, for a start I don't think, as I said, that he knew how to drive the thing. He looked very uncertain and the crew had to do an awful lot of what looked like basic instructions before he got in.'

'That's a start. One of my men's talking to them now. You seem certain of the fact that it's an accident. Why?'

'I don't know. There are lots of motives for people killing Maidenhead, but as yet I don't see motives for killing Abney. Sorry.'

'All right. What about Maidenhead? Did you find out any more? Could the same man have killed both?'

'I suppose so. If you insist Abney was murdered.'

'Have to think of everything.'

'Well, Abney might have killed Maidenhead.'

'Ah. That *would* be tidy. But why?'

'He wanted to take Maidenhead over and Maidenhead wasn't having it.'

'I don't like it but I'll buy it for now. So then what? Who killed Abney?'

'Must someone have killed him?' It had grown quite quiet now. Bognor felt life was becoming unreasonably complicated.

'Darling, are you busy?' It was Monica.

'I'm sorry, Miss,' said Smith, 'but yes.'

'See you back at the house then,' she said, 'I'll get packed.'

'Right-o.' Bognor sucked his teeth. 'Maybe it

was suicide. Perhaps he couldn't live with his guilt.'

'Did he behave like a man who was about to commit suicide?'

'I don't know. He was a good actor.'

'Hardly an ideal way to commit suicide. Nasty messy explosion in front of your wife and friends and all the papers, and taking the captain of the *Queen Ann* with you at the same time. Hardly likely.'

'He was always a showman.'

'Did anyone have a chance to tamper with the boat? Other than Abney himself?'

'The crew. And old Basil Lydeard asked if he could have a look at her before the opening.'

'And did he?'

'I don't know, but he couldn't have done much. The crew were there all the time. Besides he wouldn't know the first thing about steam engines.'

'Sure?'

'Fairly. He doesn't know much about anything.'

'Anybody else?'

'Could have been any of us,' said Bognor. 'I'm sure if I'd tipped the attendant yesterday he'd have let me look under the tarpaulin. It wasn't closely guarded. At least not to Abney's personal friends.'

'Funny lot of friends, if you ask me,' said Smith. 'Right, that'll do for now. Where can I get you?'

Bognor gave him phone numbers and went in search of Monica. He found her in their room. She looked shaken still. 'I didn't like that,' she said. 'Let's go home.'

'Nor did I,' he said, squeezing her hand. He moved to the window and looked across Cock Marsh. The police had cordoned off the bank but large crowds had gathered and were pushing against the police and gazing moronically at the house. Bognor remembered the morning's interlopers and wondered if they were there. There was even an ice-cream salesman.

'Ghouls!' he said, with distaste.

'Not really,' said Monica. 'Just people. They're curious that's all. I wonder what they expect to see.'

'Smith thinks it was murder.'

'Do you?'

'I don't know. Do you?'

'It's a bit too close to the other thing, isn't it? And after your being pushed in the river ... Oh, by the way, Mercer came with a message from Lady Abney.'

'Saying?'

'Saying, would you believe, that she was extremely sorry for any inconvenience that had been caused, that she was afraid she was going to be away for a short while with friends but that she hoped people would stay on as

124

planned, treat the house as their own and that the staff would be at their service.'

'You don't magine she meant it?'

'I should think so.'

'That really is carrying the stiff upper lip to an extreme.'

'Yes.'

Bognor chewed *his* lip and looked at her. 'You don't want to stay on, do you?'

'No, of course not.'

'Do you imagine any of the others will?'

'Some of them do seem particularly insensitive,' she said, 'I wouldn't put it past them.' She looked round the room, at the drink-filled fridge, the Pipers, the Bradley and the bottle of Balenciaga. 'Pity,' she smiled wistfully, 'I was looking forward to a touch of high living.'

Downstairs in the hall there was a row of expensive leather luggage. Bognor read the labels on each pile. No one was staying on.

CHAPTER SEVEN

All next day Bognor worked on his report. He made lists, he chewed pencils, he cudgelled his mind and he drank endless cups of coffee. Monica made the coffee and read the Sunday papers, where the late Sir Canning had

125

exceeded even the optimistic predictions of the public relations executives at Inter-communiplan. Occasionally she would read passages out to Bognor, partly for information, partly for amusement.

'Three suspect foul play, two accidental death, and two undecided,' she said, curled up in the most comfortable armchair. And this one says, "Does a sinister fiend lurk in the leafy glades and peaceful pastures of England's tranquil Thames Valley?"' She read on. 'Doesn't seem to know,' she said eventually. 'Pretty tame stuff.' Bognor chewed silently on his remaining inch of HB pencil.

'Listen,' she said. 'This one must have been in the booze tent when it happened. '"I watch as baronet and seadog perish in Thames tragedy ... One second it was a cheerful, happy Saturday afternoon with dolly girls and celebrities thronging the stately grounds of the hundred-year-old Abney House ... the next it was grief and confusion as death struck in the blazing inferno they called the Thames yesterday. As Sir Canning (motto, *J'ai bien servi*) Abney turned his magnificent £200,000 steamship *Lysander* towards shore, the ship erupted in a holocaust of destruction..."'

'Do be quiet,' pleaded Bognor, 'I'm trying to concentrate.'

They went to the pub round the corner for lunch and had sandwiches and beer.

'Just think,' said Monica, who seemed to have recovered from her shock. 'If it hadn't been for "holocaust in river of death", we'd be having an eight-course lunch, with wines to match.'

'Well, we aren't,' said Bognor, spearing a sausage. 'I think it may have been suicide. Perhaps he knew he had an incurable disease as well as having killed Freddie Maidenhead.'

'Now who's being flippant?' said Monica peevishly. She had been ticked off several times for her improper attitude.

'I'm being perfectly serious,' said Bognor, 'I'm just rather perplexed, that's all.'

By mid-afternoon he had become extremely irritable.

'Your friend Smith says every possibility is being considered,' said Monica. 'He says he is unable to rule out foul play and he says there could conceivably be a connection between the death of the Earl of Maidenhead and the deaths of Sir Canning Abney and Captain McAvity.'

'Bugger Smith,' said Bognor.

She went for a walk in the park. When she got back he had started typing, but all the same he didn't finish it till ten that night. He said he wanted it on Parkinson's desk first thing in the morning. At last he passed it to her for comment.

'PROPOSED VISIT OF HM UMDAKA OF MANGOLO TO ABNEY SMALL SHIP EXHIBITION,' it began.

'Good God,' said Monica, 'I'd forgotten all about him.'

'He's why I was there in the first place,' said Bognor, 'I wonder if he's significant at all?'

She read on. 'In view of recent events at Abney House it is quite clear that no such visit as suggested should take place in the foreseeable future.

'A murder inquiry into the death of Frederick Earl of Maidenhead is being conducted by the local police force, and although in my opinion the inquest on Sir Canning Abney and Captain McAvity will return an open verdict, it is my considered belief, shared by the police, that the latter deaths were also the result of murder and that the murderer or murderers were the same in each case.

'As yet no clear motive can be established in either case, but in view of his Rhodesian connections, a political motive could account for the first murder. If so it would appear likely that the Hon. Anstruther Grithbrice and Miss Honeysuckle Johnson might be involved, as both are known Mangolan and African nationalist sympathizers. I am not aware that Sir Canning was politically involved, but I cannot emphasize too strongly that suspects must include the staff of Abney House and Abney enterprises; and that security is extremely lax. This is largely inevitable since the River Thames which flows past the house and grounds is, in effect, a public thoroughfare.'

Monica looked up. 'Turn that down, would you?' she said. (Bognor had put on a record of massed pipes and drums.) 'You don't really think it was one of the staff?'

'Never liked the look of Mercer. Peter Williams must be a possible.'

'Why?'

'We've discussed all this.'

'Only in relation to Maidenhead.'

'Well, he wanted Abney dead so he could run the business all on his own.'

'Who would inherit?'

'Isobel Abney presumably. No children.'

'Cosmo Green would get his debts back.'

'Yes.' He smiled at her. 'I have to put that bit in to make sure they don't send him there.'

'Might they?'

'Not unless they want him knocked off.'

'But they might want him knocked off.'

'True enough,' he conceded, 'but surely not here. I mean the Umdaka may be a bloody nuisance alive in Mangolo, but he'd be even more of a nuisance dead in Buckinghamshire.'

'All right. Let me finish it. There's not a lot more.' She read on for a few minutes, frowning. 'It's not very conclusive,' she said finally.

'I suggest he should go to see Lord Montagu's motor cars instead, and the maritime

129

museum at Buckler's Hard. That's pretty conclusive.'

'I don't mean about what we should do with the Umdaka; I mean about who's guilty.'

'That's not my brief. Officially, anyway. Besides I don't feel conclusive about guilt. In fact, I haven't the first idea about it. The more I think about it the less conclusive I get. It's Smith's job not mine.'

'That depends.'

'On what?'

'On what Parkinson says among other things.'

Bognor's report was on Parkinson's desk at eight-thirty and Bognor was summoned by him at eight-thirty-five. Parkinson was still scrutinizing it when he arrived. He stood waiting, uncomfortably aware of the gaze of Her Majesty the Queen from the official regulation photograph behind Parkinson's desk.

'You had an interesting weekend,' said Parkinson, looking up. 'Sit down. Tell me more. Have a cup of tea. How do the other half live, eh? How do the other half die?'

Bognor was basically frightened of Parkinson, but he drew spurious comfort from the notion that his aggression stemmed from an inferiority complex. Unlike him, Parkinson had never been to university, nor had the benefit of a formal education after the age of fourteen.

'You agree with my conclusion?'

'What conclusion?'

'That the Umdaka shouldn't go to Abney.'

Parkinson looked at his subordinate with an expresson of infinite weariness. 'Frankly,' he said, 'I wouldn't advise my little old granny to go to Abney, even if she went in an armour-plated charabanc with the 3rd Parachute Regiment. Your friends would still find some way of dealing with her.'

Bognor remained silent and looked at the Queen. Parkinson returned to the report. 'I should say,' he said, 'that this was a verbose and pompous statement of the obvious. Naturally I will not have the Umdaka wandering round the Thames Valley while every idiot aristocrat in the country attempts to murder him. I had already decided that. What I want to know is: one, was Maidenhead murdered for political reasons? Two, was Abney murdered for political reasons? If so by whom? These are simple questions and they should be simply answered. They require the answers "yes" or "no" in the first two cases and they require one name in the last instance. That is all. Do I make myself clear?'

'Yes. Very.'

'Good. I'm glad.' He paused and sipped tea. 'To be absolutely honest,' he said, mellowing slightly, 'I did not want to expose you to this sort of situation after that disastrous affair of the friars, and when I sent you down to

131

investigate the Umdaka's visit I had no idea . . .
however, now that you're involved in it, I'm
afraid you will have to stay involved. It's not
what I would have wished but I see no
alternative.'

'Surely it could be left to the police?'

'It is being left to the police. You will simply
liaise with the police. Please try to remember
that your interests are political. Try to leave the
dramatics to the police. I don't want to find you
on the front pages of the papers. I don't want
complaints about you. I just want an
unobtrusive presence.'

'What about the police? Are they agreeable?'

'Oddly enough, they suggested it. Man
named Smith, backed by his Chief Constable.
Said you seemed to have infiltrated very
adroitly.'

Bognor smiled. 'So someone appreciates me?'

'I put them right on that. I told them it was
simply a matter of class and education.'

'Thank you very much.'

'Now.' Parkinson shuffled some papers on his
desk. 'This could become mildly embarrassing.
At least, if this means anything and isn't
someone's idea of a practical joke. Foreign
Office passed this over.' He waved a piece of
paper which bore the warning 'Immediate—by
hand at all stages'. 'It appears that some
Mangolan nationalist organization in
conjunction with the "Pan African Liberation

Corps"'—he glanced up at Bognor, 'mean anything?' to which Bognor shook his head—'have claimed responsibility for shooting the Earl of Maidenhead.'

'Ah.' Bognor wondered if it could have emanated from Grithbrice and Johnson. 'You were right about the Johnson girl,' he said. 'If that's a genuine claim then it obviously implicates Johnson and Grithbrice.'

'Do you believe IRA claims and PLA claims and Black September claims?'

'Not always.'

'Well, I never believe them,' said Parkinson firmly. 'It's our job not to believe anything anyone else claims until we have proved it. So pay no attention to this claim unless you can prove, and I mean prove, that the girl Johnson or the man Grithbrice actually did it. And when you do prove it don't go charging around making a fool of yourself. Tell me and tell Smith and we'll let the police do it properly.'

Bognor turned to go, but before he did, Parkinson said, placatory once more: 'Do you really have no idea who might have done it? Done them?'

Bognor took a deep breath. 'In my opinion, sir, it could have been Sir Archibald McCrum of that ilk, Lady McCrum, the Marquis of Lydeard, the Hon. Anstruther Grithbrice, Miss Honeysuckle Johnson, Lady Abney, Lady Maidenhead, Peter Williams or Cosmo Green.

And the Earl of Maidenhead could have been shot by Sir Canning Abney. Or the butler, Mercer, might have done it.'

'Oh, good,' said Parkinson, 'I'm delighted to hear that you're making such swift progress.'

Outside Bognor swore vehemently and went off to the library. He would start again at the beginning by looking out the file on each suspect and both corpses. He had dismissed the thought that the Saturday explosion was intended to kill Captain McAvity and not Abney, but it recurred suddenly. Reluctantly he added the thought to all the others.

Three hours later after a lengthy study of the files and of Debrett's and Burke's he was immersed in irrelevant coats of arms, courant dragons and tigers proper, dead dowagers, cousins in council houses and unheard-of titles covering every part of the country from Orkney to Padstow. He had learnt that most of them were multiple car owners: Abney, a Rolls, a Mercedes, two Toyota Estate cars and a Mini Cooper; Maidenhead had had a Rolls, Lamborghini, Morgan, Range Rover and Mini Cooper; Grithbrice had a Bentley, Range Rover, Porsche and Mini Cooper; Green had four Aston Martins; McCrum a Daimler, two Land Rovers and a Rover 3-litre; Lydeard a 1928 Lagonda and a Ford Escort. The first four had personalized number plates: CAB 1 for Abney, M 1 for Maidenhead, GRI 1 for

Grithbrice and CG 1 for Cosmo Green. All, of course, had vast estates, though only Grithbrice, or rather his father, had two stately homes—apart from Netherly there was a castle on Sutherland—but all except Lydeard and McCrum had places abroad. Abney on Corfu, Maidenhead on Sardinia, Grithbrice in Provence and Green in the south of Italy.

Under 'politics' he learnt that all except Grithbrice were conservatives and pillars of local associations. Grithbrice appeared to have played around with innumerable beliefs in a candy-floss way, but had never stuck for long.

Each one, as he already knew, retained large personal staffs. Even the McCrum, who seemed the most impoverished, managed a chauffeur, a housekeeper, two gardeners, four ghillies, a bailiff, and 'numerous domestics and entertainment staff retained on a part-time or temporary basis'. One man, Mercer, was mentioned by name, 'Mercer,' he read, 'Major James Mercer, MC and bar, butler to Sir Canning Abney for fifteen years, served with distinction in Special Operations Executive in Occupied France 1940–5. Drinks.' That, conceded Bognor, was interesting if hardly relevant.

Lydeard and McCrum had been at Eton. Lydeard had followed with Christchurch, McCrum with Sandhurst and the Scots Guards. Abney had been at Harrow and Trinity Hall,

Cambridge; Maidenhead, Eton and New College, Oxford. Grithbrice had been at Millfield, Le Rosay (Switzerland), Trinity (Cambridge), Perugia and Yale. Oddly not one of them had any children and Mr Green, of course, had no education whatever, although in the matter of company directorships he outstripped the others with ridiculous ease.

There was no file on Williams, and nothing of any interest on Captain McAvity. Of the wives, Dora Maidenhead had evidently been some sort of model though it was not clear what; Isobel Abney was the fifth daughter of the seventeenth Earl of Ormskirk and had, as Bognor knew, been a famous beauty; Mabel McCrum came from a naval family and her father had ended his career at the Royal Naval College at Dartmouth. 'Honeysuckle' Johnson's file told him nothing that he didn't know already except that she had been involved (although nothing was officially proved) in an abortive hi-jack operation in Wyoming two years previously.

All were marked down as extravagantly rich, though in terms of possessions rather than cash. Lydeard had his Canalettos and bison; Abney his museum and a fine collection of modern paintings; Maidenhead magnificent family silver and porcelain, Van Dycks, animals; Grithbrice—or rather Arborfield—more animals, Turners and tapestry. Even the McCrum boasted the world's finest collection of hunting knives, an important display of stuffed wildlife and an unequalled collection of Landseers. Only Cosmo Green managed liquidity and income to any massive degree. He 'advised' seventeen major companies on fiscal matters and was chairman of three more; he held shares amounting to several million pounds. In addition he owned Hook, arguably the finest country house in the country, indeed, if you admired Vanbrugh's work, probably the finest in the world. Green had stuffed it with Picassos and Constables. It appeared they were the only two painters of whom he had heard. The library alone was insured for a million pounds. Bognor was surprised. He knew he was rich, but not *that* rich.

Nevertheless, as far as murder was concerned, there was depressingly little. There was nothing even to suggest a political motive for murdering Abney. Apart from his presidency of the local Conservative Association he had no politics, and even the most rabid Marxist could scarcely make such a position the pretext for murder. As well assassinate Sir Tufton Beamish or Sir Clive Bossom.

He had assembled all this half-relevant information in his customary list and was staring at it dejectedly when a secretary came into the library and motioned to him to come to the telephone.

'Someone called Smith,' she said, 'from

Maidenhead. I asked if you could ring him back but he said it was urgent. I hope you don't mind.'

Bognor said it was perfectly all right. He was feeling put upon.

'Morning,' said Smith. 'You were right about Lydeard.'

'What about Lydeard?'

'He had a look at the *Lysander* that afternoon before the explosion. The crew say he was on board for about five minutes and they left him alone for about two of them.'

'That was careless.'

'You can hardly blame them, the man's a buffoon.'

'So you don't think he had anything to do with it?'

'Well, apart from the conspicuous absence of motive, he doesn't know the first thing about steam engines. Anyhow, the crew would have noticed if anything was wrong.'

'Would they?'

'Well, you have a point there. Neither of them seemed to know much more about the workings of the *Lysander* than your friend Sir Canning and that was precisely nil.'

'So it looks like accident again.'

'I'm not so sure about that. It's what I was ringing about. Can you meet me in Gray's Inn in an hour?'

'Why?'

'I've had a call from Sir Canning's solicitor. He says there's something he has to tell us. I thought, since you're, as they say, "liaising" with us, you might as well come too.'

They arranged to meet in the Blue Lion in Gray's Inn Road, and Bognor decided to walk over. It was a fine day and it would take no more than half an hour from Whitehall. He tidied up and strolled across St James's Park, stopped on the bridge to watch the flamingoes and the casually-dressed morning strollers, raced up the Duke of York's steps two at a time. At Piccadilly he bought a *Standard* and saw that the Mangolan claim had made the front page. 'Rebel exiles claim Maidenhead death' it said, but it was not the lead story, and it was extremely vague, based on an *Agence France Presse* report. He very much doubted whether anyone would bother to send a reporter to Algiers to find out more, though it was conceivable that someone might get on to Grithbrice and Johnson. He wondered if these revelations were going to mean the end of a beautiful friendship.

Smith was waiting in the Blue Lion when he got there, sipping at a half pint of bitter and reading the *Standard*.

'Did your people know about this?' he asked, pointing to the Algiers story.

'Naturally,' said Bognor.

'Taking it seriously?'

139

'Not unless we can prove anything.'

'It would mean the Johnson girl and that Grithbrice character,' said Smith. 'Grithbrice had so many motives it's ridiculous. I have an idea that Cumberledge is going to give us another in a few minutes.'

'Cumberledge?'

'Cumberledge is Abney's old solicitor, the one we're going to see.'

'What's it about?'

'He wouldn't discuss it over the phone. I pushed him a bit and he said something about Abney having been to see him last week. Said it concerned Anstruther Grithbrice and Cosmo Green.'

'We haven't had those two names bracketed together before.'

'No we have not.'

Bognor swilled some of his half-pint round in his mouth and thought for a moment. 'What do you think about a conspiracy theory?' he asked.

'I don't,' said Smith flatly.

They finished the beer and walked round the corner to an elegant eighteenth-century terrace where Cumberledge, Cumberledge, Cumberledge and Smithers had their offices. The interior was as elegantly Georgian as the outside, and so in his way was Mr Cumberledge senior. His office was on the first floor, an amply proportioned room with a large mahogany desk littered with papers tied with

140

pink ribbon. Books lined three corners of the room and Bognor noticed Dicey, Halsbury, and Salmond on torts. The fourth wall, behind Mr Cumberledge's highbacked leather-upholstered chair, was largely window and gave a pleasant view of the similar terrace on the other side of the street. Mr Cumberledge rose stiffly, and came round the desk revealing dark striped trousers below his black coat.

'Good day, gentlemen, good day.' He was a man of about sixty, with a dry lined face, a thin mouth and gold-rimmed glasses. He wore a red rose in his buttonhole, and had done every day of his working life. He grew them.

'You'll take a glass of sherry, I trust.' He went to an occasional table and poured three glasses from a decanter, which dated from the same period as the house, and gave one to each of them. He then returned to his chair, motioned his guests to sit, and took off the glasses, which he started to polish with his pocket handkerchief. When they were cleaned to his satisfaction he returned them to his nose, adjusted them and sifted some papers. Then he took them off and addressed his audience, now in precisely the agony of suspense which the operation had been intended to produce.

'Well, gentlemen, no doubt you are asking why I asked you to come to see me?'

There seemed to Bognor to be no need for an answer, and neither he nor Smith gave one.

'As I told you on the telephone, I am the legal representative of the late Sir Canning Abney—indeed my family have represented the Abneys for a number of generations.' He coughed, and continued, 'Now what I am about to tell you must please remain in the very strictest confidence at this stage. I hope I have your agreement on that point.' He looked from one to the other of them and waited until they nodded in agreement. 'You will understand why in a moment. It could be said that I am acting unethically but after giving the matter the greatest possible consideration, especially with regard to the unfortunate circumstances surrounding the death of the deceased I find that I am left with no alternative.' Again he paused, and for a moment the only sound in the room was the gentle tick of the gilt carriage clock on the marble mantelpiece beneath the (very bad) portrait of the first John Cumberledge.

The present Mr Cumberledge picked up a piece of paper and read it for a moment. 'This is Sir Canning's last will and testament—of which incidentally I am the sole executor—but before I divulge the contents of this I had better return to the circumstances of its commission.

'Last week, on the Tuesday, Sir Canning came to see me, by arrangement. He seemed to me in a condition of some distress. I must impress on you, by the way, that I tell you this

142

not only because I believe it to be my duty to assist the course of justice, but also because I consider myself still bound by my obligations to my late client.'

Bognor was consumed with boredom. He noticed Smith look at his watch. Cumberledge, though he gave no sign of it, must have noticed.

'To be brief, gentlemen, he wanted to change his will. His previous will, you understand, left everything to Lady Abney. However, it seems that he had lately become cognizant of some . . . er, marital infidelity on her part. Although I understand he had no wish to pursue the matter during his lifetime in view of the unfortunate publicity and distress such action might cause he nevertheless felt it wrong to leave the estate to Lady Abney. There are, I should say, certain insurance policies in her name, which still stand. There is no question whatever of Lady Abney being left destitute. Sir Canning made certain disclosures of a sexual nature, which frankly I do not feel I should repeat.'

Bognor moved nearer the edge of his chair. This was interesting.

'There were two crucial points,' continued Mr Cumberledge, in a voice which was utterly devoid of emotion. 'First of all, Sir Canning wished the small ships museum and Abney House itself to remain open to the public and to continue to be run in precisely the same way as hitherto. As you probably know, he had no issue and he felt that neither Lady Isobel nor his younger brother, Grafton, could be relied upon to carry out his wishes in this respect. He therefore willed the entire organization with all the contents to ...' Bognor had a distinct impression that Mr Cumberledge was enjoying this much more than he should. Mr Cumberledge squinted at the document, and looked up smiling slightly, 'To the Honourable Anstruther Grithbrice of Netherly, Staffordshire.' He put down his glasses and regarded Bognor and Smith with an expression of malicious anticipation. 'In view, as I say, of the unfortunate occurrences of last weekend, I felt that this was something which should be brought to your attention ... A little more sherry?'

He collected the decanter, poured three more measures and this time left the decanter on his desk.

'That's extremely interesting, sir, but in view ...' Mr Cumberledge waved Smith down with an admonitory hand. 'I need hardly say, that the interested parties have already been apprised of the contents of Sir Canning's will. There are also, of course, the usual small bequests to personal friends and members of the staff, but these need not concern us at the moment. However,' he said the word with renewed emphasis, '*however*, that is not all. As I have already intimated, Sir Canning seemed to me to be in a state of no little agitation, if not distress. I naturally attribute this in part to his discovery of Lady Abney's er, indiscretion, but I also formed the opinion that this was not in itself anything very new, and that he had simply had confirmation of something that he had suspected for no little time. I understand also that the matter of leaving the estate to Mr Grithbrice arose in part from some business discussions the two men had already had, and that this could have been more important than any feeling of antipathy towards Lady Abney, which in any case he did not entirely feel. As I mentioned earlier Sir Canning made a number of confessions of a really highly embarrassing nature.' He sipped at his sherry, and took a cigarette from the silver box in front of him, offering one as an afterthought to his guests who both declined.

'To continue,' he said, 'it seems that Sir Canning had been threatened by a person named Green, to whom he owed money.'

'But,' interjected Bognor, 'there wasn't much involved, surely.'

Mr Cumberledge pushed his glasses to the end of his nose and looked at Bognor as if he was an impertinent and ill-informed schoolboy.

'It really depends, Mr Bognor, what you mean by the idea of "not very much". The sum involved may not seem very much to people like yourself or Mr Green, but to people like the late

145

Sir Canning and myself it seemed a very great deal indeed.'

'How much?'

'Just one moment,' while once more Cumberledge fiddled with his papers. Bognor, who had decided the whole act was a charade was irritated again.

'Here we are,' said Mr Cumberledge, studying it carefully. 'It seems a very great deal of money to me, Mr Bognor, but perhaps the pay in Whitehall is rather higher than I had imagined, eh?' He chuckled humourlessly. 'The sum which Mr Green was claiming from Sir Canning was two hundred and seventeen thousand, three hundred and forty pounds, twenty-five and a half pence.'

There was a silence, during which the carriage clock, with much winding and whirring struck the half-hour. Then Bognor said, 'I'm sorry. I knew that Sir Canning owed money to Mr Green but I'd no idea it was so much. But what do you mean that he was threatened by Green?'

'I'm not absolutely certain what form the threats took, but I understand it was connected in some way with Pring's.'

'His club?'

'That is correct, yes.'

'What exactly was the connection?' asked Smith.

Cumberledge looked knowing. 'Sir Canning

146

was, as I say, more than a little distressed and there were other more important matters to resolve than the question of Mr Green and Pring's. However, although I am not a trained detective,' here he allowed himself a little smirk, 'I deduced that Mr Green was prepared to reduce his claim in return for election to Pring's. Sir Canning was, as you are no doubt aware, on the committee of the club just as his father had been.'

'And Sir Canning refused?'

'So I would presume.'

'And then what?'

'Mr Green, I understand had become most threatening.'

'Do you understand that he had threatened violence?' Smith looked amazed by the whole idea.

'Not exactly, no. I understood that it would have been in the form, possibly, of some form of legal action—or, more insidiously, I think you will agree, some form of whispering campaign to the effect that Sir Canning's financial situation was not quite what it might appear to casual scrutiny.'

'Nasty,' said Bognor.

'If true,' said Smith.

'I assure you, Mr Smith,' said Mr Cumberledge, his thin mouth freezing in disapproval, 'that I have no reason to lie to you.'

Smith was embarrassed. 'That's not what I meant. I only meant that Sir Canning might have been confused about Mr Green's exact intentions.'

'Ah. That I allow is conceivable, although in many years of dealing with Sir Canning's affairs I had always found him to be a man of the utmost precision.'

'Was there,' asked Bognor, 'any suggestion that Green was one of those with whom Lady Abney,' he found himself slipping uneasily into the legal vernacular, 'had formed a, how shall we put it, liaison?'

'I think not,' said Mr Cumberledge, his smile showing real malice for once. 'I understood that Mr Green's sexual proclivities lay in quite other directions. Indeed, Sir Canning taxed him with it.'

'Oh,' Bognor thought for a moment, 'what exactly were the nature of the sexual revelations which Sir Canning afforded you?'

'Gentlemen, I really am most sorry but that is something I feel it would be utterly improper for me to divulge.'

'It could be most relevant, couldn't it, Mr Smith?' Bognor turned to his colleague for support.

'Indeed it could,' agreed Smith. 'Most definitely.'

'Was Sir Canning saying that he was homosexual himself?' asked Bognor.

'That, sir, is the most disgraceful allegation. I must ask you to withdraw.' Mr Cumberledge seemed genuinely scandalized.

'I'm frightfully sorry,' said Bognor at once. 'It wasn't intended as an allegation, but naturally I withdraw immediately.'

'Look, Mr Cumberledge,' said Smith, 'you've been extremely helpful. More than helpful I should say, and if I might say so, I don't think you should trouble your conscience about having come to us—even if other members of your profession might have behaved differently.' He paused significantly. 'But you really must allow us to judge what may help us apprehend the guilty party. You simply cannot tell us that Sir Canning imparted evidence to you, evidence which may very well be material to the case in hand, and then withhold that evidence on grounds of taste or morality or whatever.'

Mr Cumberledge pushed back his chair and placed the fingertips of his hands together, contemplating them in apparent cogitation. Then he said, 'Very well, gentlemen. Sir Canning intimated to me that he had, how shall I put it, lost interest. Those indeed were his very words, "lost interest".'

'I'm sorry,' said Smith, 'I may be being extremely stupid, but lost interest in Lady Abney or what?'

'Surely you are not suggesting that, as they

149

say nowadays, you were born yesterday, Mr Smith. What I am trying to tell you is that Sir Canning had lost all interest in the sexual act, and had been unable to conjure up any particular enthusiasm for it for some time previously. I hope that satisfies you. I cannot conceive of any way in which that could be of the slightest relevance to the matter in hand.'

'I would dispute that, Mr Cumberledge, I really would,' said Smith, 'I'm sorry to say that in this case the sexual appetites of the principal protagonists may have a great deal to do with the final solution.'

'And if it's any consolation,' said Bognor, 'your late client is the only figure in the business who doesn't seem to be or to have been chronically oversexed.' He wished he hadn't said it the minute he uttered the words.

'Did Mr Grithbrice know, that Sir Canning had changed his will in his favour?' asked Smith, attempting to change the subject.

Mr Cumberledge glared at Bognor. 'I'm bound to say, sir, that I find your approach to this matter frivolous to a degree.' He turned to Smith. 'I understood that Sir Canning intended to tell Mr Grithbrice what was in his mind. I even understood that there was to be some sort of reciprocal arrangement.' He pulled a gold hunter from his waistcoat pocket, and consulted it with a frown. 'I'm sorry, gentlemen. I have another appointment for which I am already overdue. I have told you all I know and I trust that it will assist you in seeing that justice is done—though I have my misgivings in certain respects. So, gentlemen, if you will forgive me, I must bid you good-day.'

★　　　★　　　★

'Sanctimonious old bastard,' said Smith out in the street. 'He couldn't wait to tell us about Abney's sex life. Come on, I'll buy you a beer.'

They walked back to the pub in silence.

'It does begin to look like Grithbrice or Green,' said Bognor, when they had settled into a corner seat away from the bar.

'All right, tell me why.' Smith said it in a patronizing way, though Bognor had to concede that he was a deal less patronizing than Parkinson.

'Grithbrice might kill Maidenhead for his, and his girl friend's political reasons, and the fact that he wouldn't join in the new business could push him into it. Once he was dead the estate would have to pay death duties and would be less effective as a rival anyway. And he would kill Abney because he was going to succeed to the whole shooting match.'

'To coin a phrase,' said Smith, inevitably.

'And Green would kill Abney because he owed him a lot of money and because he wouldn't get him into Pring's.'

151

'Two hundred thousand is nothing to a man like Green.'

'Maybe, but getting into Pring's is. There isn't even a Rothschild in Pring's. He'd be the first of his kind. It would be a sensation.'

'All right, why kill Maidenhead?'

'He owed him money too.'

'I didn't know that. Anyway he could afford to let it stand.'

'Probably trying to force him into some deal too. I don't know. Still, you must admit, those two look the most likely.'

Smith looked arch. 'When you've been in this business as long as I have,' he said, 'you get very unhappy when too much suspicion builds up against too few people. It means things are being overlooked.' He ordered another round of beer and shook his head over it. 'All this gas. They don't brew beer like they used to. I suppose some people would have brought Grithbrice in by now; but he's a smart fellow. We have enough motives but we don't have any facts whatever. None whatever.'

'Won't the wreck show anything?' asked Bognor.

'Apart from a few bits off the hull they haven't found anything more than about an inch long. Our forensic people don't think there's an earthly. They're so desperate they've even called in a professor from the Science Museum and I've never known them do anything like that before.'

'And the bodies?'

'No bodies worth talking about. We've had some things put in boxes but apart from a signet ring and some cufflinks and a cravat pin there's nothing to tell which belongs to who. Oh and that hat. No, it won't do.'

They continued to discuss the ramifications of the murder until shortly before closing time. Even by then they had got no further, indeed after another beer they had turned to probing each other. Bognor had merely confirmed what he had assumed, that Smith was a career policeman with a wife and two sons, both doing well, who lived in a comfortable four-bedroomed house on a new estate three miles from Bourne End and didn't expect to be promoted further if only because he did his present trouble-shooting job rather too well. If the local force had anything which didn't run in the predetermined grooves they got Smith out of bed. Smith grew vegetables and had a way with rhubarb, liked a flutter on the horses and looked forward to retirement in the country. Bognor rather liked him, and he seemed to have more respect for Bognor's university background than the appalling Parkinson.

It was well after three before he got back to the office. On the way he bought a later edition of the *Standard* and found to his relief that the 'Mangolan claim' story had been pushed off the front page by the presidential crisis in the United States. He turned inside and sighed. There at the top of the page was a photograph of Sir Archibald McCrum. Above it the story was headlined, 'Mangolan death claim row grows.'

'Now, why on earth has he got in on the act?' murmured Bognor, and began to read. 'Speculation over the murder of the Earl of Maidenhead last week has grown more confused following a remarkable statement by the Scottish landowner and showman, Sir Archibald McCrum. The fifty-five-year-old former Guards Colonel said from his home, McCrum Castle, Inverness, "I have just heard that Mangolan nationalists claim responsibility for the foul murder of the Earl of Maidenhead last Friday. I myself have suspected as much ever since the Earl's tragic death, and I believe that our own police and intelligence forces have known too. I am deeply concerned that there has been an attempt to hush the matter up for some dubious political reason, and I intend to leave no stone unturned in my efforts to see that the guilty person or persons are brought to justice."

'Colonel McCrum was referring to earlier reports from Algiers that an organization calling itself the Mangolan nationalist organization had claimed to have been behind last week's shooting, when Lord Maidenhead died at the

154

home of Sir Canning Abney, who was himself killed in a boating accident the following day. Colonel McCrum, who was a guest at Abney House at the time of the incident, refused to say any more, but he added that he intended to take the matter up with "the relevant authorities".

'The Foreign Office said in a statement, "We have no knowledge of any organization calling itself the Mangolan nationalist organization".' Bognor skimmed the rest. It was a fairly comprehensive job. They mentioned that the Umdaka was making a visit to Britain in ten days' time. They hinted that the Mangolans had suggested that Maidenhead might have been involved in high-level, low-profile negotiations with 'a white African régime'. And they even, greatly daring, mentioned, at the very end of the piece, that among other guests at Abney House, had been the Hon. Anstruther Grithbrice, playboy, stately home impresario, photographer and 'self-confessed Marxist' (not something of which Bognor was aware, though in his time Grithbrice had confessed to any number of unlikely political beliefs) and his current girl friend, the beautiful, Mangolan born Miss Honeysuckle Johnson.

Bognor wondered if they would be sued for libel, but it was probably safe. It was the same technique that the press had used during the build-up to the Profumo scandal and the Lambton affair.

155

Not for the first time he approached the office in a mood of apprehension. He waved to the commissionaire in the front hall, turned left down the door marked 'Fire Escape', and went down into the subterranean wastes of the department, with its low headroom, its bilious shade of green and its pervasive armoury of central heating pipes. When he reached his desk he found two pieces of paper. One, timed at twelve-thirty said, 'See me instantly. P.', and the other said, 'Sir Archibald McCrum has telephoned several times and says could you call him on Invercrum One, Extension Six.' Bognor sighed very deeply indeed and wished that he'd worn one of his old something ties. They gave him extra confidence in facing an angry boss.

'And what exactly do you propose doing about the Monarch of the Glen?' asked Parkinson frigidly. 'It would help if you could start by taking a normal lunch hour. This isn't the Treasury you know.'

'I was with Sir Canning Abney's solicitor.'

'I don't very much care if you were with the Queen Mother. I have had communications from your friend the McCrum of that ilk,' he looked at his pad, 'four times. I have had the Permanent Under Secretary. I have had the Minister of State's Private Secretary. I have had the Minister of State. I have had the Secretary of State's Private Secretaries—both. One after the other. And finally I have had the Secretary of State himself. He was not amused. And for your private information I am not amused either, so what are you going to do about it?'

'What would you like me to do?'

'I would like you to get this kilted bugger off all our backs as quickly as possible and let us all get on with the job that our gracious Majesty is paying us to do. That is what I would like.'

'I think he's irrelevant.'

'Listen. Anyone who can make the sort of noise he's making is not irrelevant. He appears to have been at school or in the Guards or on the board with every senior official in the civil service and diplomatic corps. Not to mention the managing directors of every national newspaper and the greater part of the 1922 Committee. I thought you said he was a backwoodsman.'

'He is.'

'Then how, in God's name, is he able to make such a bloody nuisance of himself?'

'You said it yourself. He was at Eton. He was in the Guards. He has a title.'

'This isn't 1850.'

'That's your story.' Bognor regretted his belligerence. It was the beer talking. Parkinson glowered at him.

'What exactly does he want?' asked Bognor.

'He wants an immediate arrest of Grithbrice and the Johnson girl.'

'But we have no proof. And I'm not certain

157

anyway. It could even have been McCrum himself come to that.'

Parkinson showed a flicker of interest. 'Go on,' he said. 'What do you mean by that?'

'Well,' said Bognor, taking a deep breath. 'You accept an equality of opportunity?'

'In principle.'

'He had a motive for killing Maidenhead because his wife, Mabel, was having an affair with him.'

'Are you sure?'

'Practically.'

'Well, make sure before you do anythng about it. You'd better go and see him. In fact, I promised him you would. He claims he's got conclusive proof that Grithbrice was responsible, but he won't discuss it over the telephone. So you'll have to go and see him.'

'But it's bloody miles!'

'Four hundred and ninety-seven if you go by car and take the ferry. But you're not. You're booked on the sleeper from King's Cross. Which means that you'll be at McCrum Castle in time for porridge and finnan haddies with his ilk.'

Bognor was not amused. He rang Smith who was.

'It's why we were so keen to have you,' he said. 'I can't afford to go chasing the wild geese. My expenses don't stretch that far, and I'm indispensable anyway.'

CHAPTER EIGHT

The sleeping car attendant woke him next morning at six-thirty with a small pot of British Rail tea and two anaemic biscuits. He had a mild hangover, as he and Monica had gone to a Russian restaurant in Fulham and had blinis and too much vodka. Blearily he pulled aside the blind and looked out. The train was running smoothly along the moor of Rannoch and it was raining. He could vaguely make out grey-green rock and the odd crag through the mist but the visibility was poor and the place looked desolate. The tea was cool and the biscuits uninteresting. He shivered slightly.

The previous afternoon he had telephoned Invercrum One and had spoken to Lady Mabel who had sounded relieved that he was coming. A car would be dispatched to Spean Bridge and breakfast, as Parkinson had predicted, would be waiting when he arrived. The trip was, he felt sure, a complete red herring. It would achieve nothing. As the train pounded along the eastern shore of Loch Treig he dressed slowly and shaved, peering out through the window in the direction of Stob Coire Easain, most of whose three and a half thousand feet were hidden in cloud and mist. Luckily he had brought an old riding mac, but he was going to need gumboots as well and he had an uneasy feeling that the McCrum was the sort of man who would insist on talking business over a fifteen-mile deer stalk. He was glad that the grouse season had yet to begin.

By the time they reached Spean Bridge he was tweeded-up and clean shaven, though he still suffered from a headache and a general malaise of damp and depression. Although he had only been into the public rooms of McCrum Castle and that a long time ago, he remembered it as wet, windy, wintry and gaunt. He wondered if he would be able to go back on the return sleeper, but Lady McCrum had said something about dinner and he knew that the last train left in mid-afternoon. He shuddered. No electric blankets at McCrum Castle, he bet. More like stone hot-water bottles.

Nobody else got out at Spean Bridge and the platform appeared to be deserted. He stood for a moment as the train drew out, and then, as the rain began to soak into his hair and his shoes, he trotted unenthusiastically towards the ticket office. Outside it he could see a single Land Rover parked in a large puddle. There was a man sitting in the driver's seat, motionless.

Bognor ran across to the vehicle and tapped on the window. With a considerable show of reluctance the driver opened the window and stared at him. It was a red, stubbly, boorish face, surmounted by a tweed hat with a small feather in one side of the band.

'Sorry,' said Bognor. 'Are you from McCrum Castle?'

'I am.'

'Well, I expect you've come to meet me, my name's Bognor.' He was beginning to get extremely wet. The rain was dripping off the bottom of the mac on to his knees and the puddle was soaking steadily into his suedes. The boorish person continued to look at him expressionlessly.

'Happen,' he said, enigmatically.

'Look, I don't want to seem importunate but I've just got off the train and I'm getting wet.'

'You'll be the gentleman from London.'

'Of course I'm the gentleman from London.'

'Well, there's no use standing in the rain. You'd best put the case in the back and get in.' The man made no move to assist, so Bognor, greatly irritated, did as he was told. Before he was properly in, the Land Rover started with a lurch, which almost threw Bognor into the windscreen. He said nothing. As they left the village he saw a hoarding by the side of the road. 'Have a Highland Fling. Visit McCrum Castle. Highland Wildlife Park. Historic Home of Clan McCrum. Teas. Children Half Price.' The McCrum evidently lacked the flair of his southern rivals. Even in the rain he could see that the notice was ill-designed and crudely lettered.

'Filthy day,' he said conversationally as they turned right at the commando memorial and took the main road to Fort Augustus.

'Aye.'

'Still, I expect the farmers will be pleased.'

'Happen.'

He gave up. His chauffeur drove too fast for the conditions and after a further two miles turned sharply right and started to climb a narrow, steep, single-track road, which led through fir forests. Bognor had seen no signpost and imagined it was a back entrance. After a further few minutes they came to a lodge, with open gates and a cattle grid over which they rumbled.

A mile away across a Highland apology for a park he could make out the dim grey shape of the castle. As they drew nearer he recognized it from the recesses of memory: the wild Disneylike battlements, the great banner of the McCrums flapping sodden from the flagpole, the vast wooden doors, the minute slit-like windows, the mad phoney gloom of the place. The dour driver stopped the machine in a swirl of gravel and waited. Bognor got out and, since he was clearly to get no assistance, went to the back and hauled out his case. The Land Rover drove off immediately leaving him alone before the castle gates. He walked over to them and pulled at the heavy pendulous piece of wrought iron at one side. A moment later there was a distant clang and a baying sound which denoted large dog.

He waited. A minute or so later he heard shuffling noises from within and then the sound of bolts being drawn back. Then the door was opened a couple of inches and a thin, pale-faced woman peered out at him.

'Not open this morning,' she said. 'Come back at three.'

By this time Bognor was so wet and so cross that before the door was closed again he put his foot in it.

'I've come from London to see Sir Archibald,' he said loudly.

The old woman looked unimpressed. 'They all say that,' she said. 'London, did you say?'

'Yes, London. Look, please will you let me in.'

Before she could reply, Bognor heard another noise of door-opening from within and a familiar voice called, 'That will do, thank you, Mrs Campbell. It must be Mr Bognor.'

Mrs Campbell withdrew her face from the chink in the doorway and a second later it opened a further couple of feet. It was Mabel McCrum.

'My dear Mr Bognor, I am sorry. You must be wet through. I'm so sorry. Do please come in. I'm afraid we're having a terrible time with the staff. Mrs Campbell has been with us years and years but she's quite deaf and becoming more senile by the minute. I am sorry. I think it will be safer if I show you to your room myself.'

Minutes later she left him, after a long walk through cavernous corridors, in a large chamber which gave every impression of having been hewn from the living granite. She had given him detailed directions of how to get to the morning room where breakfast was waiting, but without a map he was not optimistic. He towelled himself down and wondered if there would be lumps in the porridge. There was a fireplace in the room, but needless to say no fire. The chimney had not been blocked off and the wind sighed down it, eddying out of the grate, flicking at the bottoms of the curtains, the corners of the counterpane and increasing his sense of unhappiness. Partly dry, he set off in search of breakfast and found it with surprising ease not two minutes later. Luckily his sense of smell had not deserted him.

Lady McCrum was as dumpy and plain as he remembered her. But she was nice with it. He supposed that for Freddie Maidenhead the niceness might have been an attraction after the very obvious nastiness of his own wife, but even so the relationship seemed surprising.

'I hope you like kippers,' she said brightly. 'They come from Mallaig up the coast.'

'Very much,' he said. She pushed the bell

164

under the table with her foot, and a few minutes later a maid came in. 'Two pairs of kippers, please,' she said, 'and do ask cook not to overdo them this time.' The porridge, meanwhile, was relatively lump-free, if tepid.

'What a dreadful few days this has been,' said Lady McCrum. 'Poor Archie is absolutely beside himself with rage, but I'm afraid I just find the whole thing terribly depressing. But I expect you're always dealing with sudden death and disaster.'

'Not really,' said Bognor, 'I'm afraid most of my work is very dull. Where is your husband by the way?'

'Oh,' Lady Mabel flushed, 'how silly of me, I quite forgot to tell you. He's gone fishing. He thought he'd manage to get in a couple of hours before you arrived. I do hope he hasn't forgotten.'

Bognor looked out of the window at the rain driving across the park and hiding the hills, and winced. His worst suspicions about the McCrum were confirmed. Lady McCrum noticed.

'I'm afraid bad weather brings out the worst in Archie,' she said. 'I thought it might get better with age but if anything it's worse. Sometimes he's out all night with the ghillies. Last year when we had that dreadful blizzard he went for a swim in the loch.'

'Was that wise?'

'Not in the least. He caught a terrible cold, but he insisted it was nothing to do with the swim. He said it was the central heating. Apparently it's a well-known fact that central heating gives you colds, but as our central heating hasn't worked properly for at least fifteen years, it didn't seem awfully likely.'

The kippers arrived. Bognor pronounced them excellent.

'I'm so glad. We're rather proud of them ourselves.' She smiled at him and suddenly, to Bognor's horror, burst into tears. He went on eating his kipper and pretended not to notice. After a while she mopped herself up with her small lace handkerchief and said, 'I *am* sorry, Mr Bognor. Please forgive me. It's just that it's such a relief to have someone to talk to.'

Bognor could think of nothing very apt to say. 'Do please talk if it's any help,' he said, slightly spoiling the effect by having a mouth full of kipper.

'Archie's so insensitive about everything,' she said. 'All he's interested in is doing down Grithbrice because he thinks he's a bad show. He doesn't seem to have any regrets about what's happened.' She paused and then said nervously, 'I suppose you know about me and poor Freddie?'

'I don't *know* anything, Lady McCrum, but yes, I have heard things said.'

'It's true,' she said in a very small voice and

166

Bognor had a ghastly feeling she was going to burst into tears again. 'It's all true. I've tried to tell Archie, only he wouldn't understand and he never listens. I don't seem to be able to get near him any longer. Freddie was so gentle.'

Bognor had no wish to hear confession, not that he was lacking in sensitivity. Rather the reverse. 'I suppose,' he said, 'you have no idea about who might have done it? Murdered Lord Maidenhead, I mean.'

Lady McCrum dabbed at her eyes again. 'I don't know,' she said. 'I have two sorts of ideas, but one of them's so dreadful I can't think about it.'

'You mean,' Bognor said it as gently as he knew how, 'you mean that perhaps your husband might have done it?'

She nodded sadly, the tears cascading down her cheeks and making her make-up run. 'Yes,' she sobbed, making no attempt now to control herself. 'And whatever I think about him, I couldn't bear to lose both of them.' She gave way to incoherent sobs. Bognor made comforting noises.

'But you were with your husband all the time. You must know he couldn't have done it.'

'That's just it,' she said, between sobs. 'He said he had an upset stomach and he got up to go to the loo at about ten to seven and he took a book with him and he didn't come back for simply ages.'

'He wouldn't have gone all the way over to the shooting range, collected a .22, come back and shot Lord Maidenhead, put the rifle back in the range and come back to you, wearing his pyjamas and dressing-gown,' said Bognor, trying to inject some realism into the situation.

'You don't know Archie,' she said, dissolving into further hysterics.

Bognor got a kipper bone caught between two of his front teeth and spent some time wrestling it out. When he had done so, he said, 'I still think it's very unlikely. Do you think he might have found out about you and the Earl? I mean, it's rather odd that he hasn't said anything about it to you since.'

'He's *been* rather odd, that's just it. I'm sorry, you must think me awfully childish and silly, but I've been so upset lately. It was *The Law o' the Lariat* by Oliver Strange.'

'I'm sorry,' said Bognor, who had helped himself to toast, 'what was?'

'The book Archie took to the loo. He always reads westerns on the loo. He says it helps. He's always had trouble like that. It's been worse lately. I've always said he should try syrup of figs but he just doesn't seem to listen. He never listens.'

The tears were getting him down. 'I'm quite sure it was somebody else, Lady McCrum. There's nothing to worry about.'

She shook her head vehemently. 'I'm sure it

168

wasn't Tony Grithbrice. He and Freddie were quite close until Canning Abney started intriguing. He was always intriguing. I expect you knew that. You couldn't say something to Archie, could you?'

Bognor was perplexed. 'How do you mean?'

'About me and Freddie.'

'It's hardly my place to tell him something like that. I mean it is rather personal.'

'No,' she said, 'don't tell him anything, just find out if he knows. For all our sakes. But I'm sure he'd listen to you. You're a man.'

He didn't like the way the conversation was going, but she suddenly seemed pathetically eager and hopeful.

'I am sorry,' she said, 'I'm neglecting you terribly. Do have some more coffee. But listen, don't you see if you just mentioned it somehow in passing, while you were talking about the murders and things. I mean it could come out quite naturally, and you could treat it all as if it was terribly matter of fact and didn't threaten him in any way. Couldn't you?'

'But just suppose,' Bognor shifted his ground, 'just suppose he had found out about you and Lord Maidenhead and that he did object and went out and shot him. What then?'

'But you said you didn't think he did.'

'I don't, but I don't know.'

'You will try, won't you? Please?'

Oh God, thought Bognor, anything to stop

that terrible wailing voice and that martyred expression. Out loud he said, 'Yes, of course, Lady McCrum, I'll try. I'll do my best, I really will. Only of course it may not work.'

'Oh, thank you,' she said, with such genuine gratitude that Bognor immediately felt guilty. He drank more coffee and had another piece of toast.

'You were saying,' he said, 'that you had two sorts of ideas. What was the other?'

'The other?' She looked blank and fingered her pearls. 'You're quite right, I did say there was another and for the moment I've quite forgotten what it was.'

'Perhaps you thought someone else might have had a motive for killing the Earl of Maidenhead. Someone other than your husband.'

'Of course. That horrid Mr Green.'

'Cosmo Green?'

'Yes. He is unspeakable. I have nothing against him in principle, you understand. I mean, I'm not like that. I'm not in the least prejudiced. I know it's a cliché to say it and you'll probably laugh but some of my best friends are Jews. Really. Only Mr Green is such a Jewish little Jew. I really do think he might have killed Freddie. I really do.'

'Go on.' Bognor could see it coming. Money again. He knew that already.

'Freddie owed him two hundred thousand
170

pounds. He'd needed some new elephants and the ladies' loos had to be done up. You've no idea what women get up to in lavatories, they're far worse than men. Anyway there were all sorts of things he had to spend money on and the bank were being very difficult. You know how difficult banks can be these days. And then just when Freddie was going to take some of the silver down to Sotheby's, Mr Green came to dinner, and it all happened.'

'But with respect,' said Bognor, 'two hundred thousand pounds is nothing to Cosmo Green. If Lord Maidenhead had never repaid it I doubt if Green would have noticed. He's got millions, literally. He's richer than Getty.'

'It wasn't as simple as that,' said Lady McCrum. 'In fact it was odious, quite odious. He wanted Freddie to do things in return for the loan. He didn't say anything about it at first. Not until Freddie had bought the elephants and done the loos and everything. Then he suddenly turned round and said he wanted to go to a garden party at the Palace. Well, that was all right. Freddie got him in there without any trouble. Him *and* a friend mind you. But that wasn't all.'

She fiddled under the table for the bell and suggested they moved to her drawing-room. It turned out to be the best room so far. It was high in a turret, octagonal and had fitted floral carpet, an off-cream pekingese sat on a sofa and

171

there were family photographs everywhere.

'Rather like blackmail,' said Bognor, walking to the window and noticing with relief that the rain had stopped and the cloud cleared. The McCrum had evidently carried out a forestry programme since his last visit. The surrounding mountains were covered in small fir trees.

'It *was* blackmail. First it was the Palace garden party. Then he wanted to meet Freddie's friends. Racing people particularly, but anyone with a title seemed to do. Freddie gritted his teeth and had him to stay for a weekend, and he took him to lunch at the Turf and White's. Then Freddie and Dora went to Hook for a weekend and had the Lincolnshires and the Berkshires in. And I believe they took Mr Green to see Cynthia Worcester but Buffy Berkshire had warned her and she pretended to be out.'

Lady McCrum patted the pekingese and gave it a chocolate. 'I shouldn't really, I know,' she said, 'but we don't have many vices, do we, Cecil?'

'Go on,' said Bognor, 'I imagine it had got worse recently.'

'Yes. In the last few weeks. Freddie was stalling like mad but it was becoming most embarrassing. First of all he said he wanted to give Princess Anne a horse. Well, Freddie explained that you didn't do things like that and that you had to have met them first at the very least. So then Mr Green said he'd like to meet her in that case, and Freddie explained very patiently that he didn't know the princess and the only one he knew was her father because he played polo with him, and he said anyway they didn't get on because Freddie swore at him once in Greek and apparently the prince didn't like it. Anyway the next thing was Green said he wanted to get into parliament and he understood the local constituency near Hook belonged to the Lincolnshires and how much would they want for it. Again Freddie had to explain that Mark, the Lincolnshires' eldest, had the seat and would go on being the MP until his father died, and then probably he'd give it to *his* son. And Freddie said wouldn't Mr Green be better off with the Labour people, they were more his sort. That didn't go down at all well I gather. There was rather a scene and next day Green rang back and told Freddie he wanted a peerage. I mean, imagine!'

'So what did Lord Maidenhead do?'

'Well,' Lady McCrum's handkerchief came out again, 'he didn't have a great deal of alternative by then. Mr Green was talking about demanding the money back immediately. So he said he'd do what he could but it would take time. And from then on ...' Her voice started to break. 'From then on, until the day he died, hardly a day passed without Mr Green making horrid threatening noises about his wretched

173

peerage.'

Bognor sighed. 'He should have told him to get stuffed, like Canning Abney.'

Lady McCrum stopped sniffing and looked up. 'What do you mean?'

'He did exactly the same with Canning Abney. Lent him over two hundred thousand, and then asked to be made a member of Pring's.'

'Goodness.' For the first time that morning Lady McCrum laughed. 'Mr Green. Pring's. How awful.'

She laughed again. It was rather a pleasant sound and Bognor again had a glimpse of what Freddie Maidenhead had seen in her. Then she realized the implication of what she'd heard.

'Goodness,' she said again, 'and Canning refused point blank. Then what happened?'

'There was a scene. I understand Mr Green became abusive and threatening.'

Lady McCrum looked very thoughtful and patted the pekingese.

'So,' she said, 'Mr Green was demanding favours from Freddie and Canning. And Freddie, poor lamb, wasn't able to do anything about the peerage. And Canning refused to do anything about Pring's. And they both died one after the other. And Mr Green was staying in the house at the same time.'

They sat in silence. Bognor wishing he hadn't had the second piece of toast, and Lady

174

McCrum stroking Cecil.

'Do you really think ...?' she asked.

'I don't know what to think,' he said, 'but it's beginning to look very like it.'

★   ★   ★

A further quarter of an hour elapsed and still Sir Archibald had not returned. Bognor once more said that he would see what he could do about mentioning Lady McCrum's relationship with Lord Maidenhead, and naturally, added that he would do everything in his power to stop the McCrum making more of an ass of himself than he already had. Lady McCrum, who was now insisting that Bognor call her Mabel, said she would assist over this, but that it would be difficult. Once Archie got an idea fixed in what passed for his mind it stayed fixed.

As the weather was brightening they decided to go in search of the highland chief. Bognor put on his riding mac, borrowed a pair of gum boots and a tweed hat of a similar type to the one worn by the Land Rover driver; and Mabel McCrum put on a duffel coat over her McCrum kilt. They set off across the park at a brisk pace.

'Those are the animals,' she said, waving her walking stick in the direction of some heavily-wired stockades behind which a mangy pair of lupine creatures were pacing hungrily. 'We only have animals which come originally from the Highlands. Those are wolverine. We have wolves and snow leopard and lynx and beavers too. Archie's going to try to get the beavers to build a dam but they're not being frightfully cooperative. He's just started negotiating for an elk.'

'Not with funds borrowed from Cosmo Green, I hope,' said Bognor flippantly, realizing with a sudden shock that Green had claimed to have lent money to the McCrum.

'Oh, I do hope not,' said Lady McCrum, laughing, 'I don't think it's very likely. Archie never discusses money but he's very clever about it. You could say he was rather mean, and I'm sure he'd never borrow from a man like Mr Green. Archie's a great believer in protocol.'

Bognor decided to say no more. The McCrum marital situation was fraught enough as it was.

'I hope you're fairly fit,' she said, lengthening her stride, 'I have a feeling we'll find him down at the Ghillies' Tomb.'

Bognor winced, and her ladyship, who was obviously in first-class physical trim, proceeded to tell him, in gory detail, precisely how the Ghillies' Tomb got its name when, in 1824, a previous McCrum had come upon two of his own ghillies attempting to poach salmon from a stretch of river with a pool and waterfall which was a particular favourite of his, and famous throughout the Highlands for its fish. The

McCrum had immediately conducted a brisk interrogation and when, after some thirty seconds, he had established the men's guilt beyond question, he had made them stand at the edge of the fall, and discharged both barrels of his shotgun into them from close range.

'I sometimes think Archie's a bit like that,' said Lady McCrum, 'I'm sure that's what he'd like to do to Tony Grithbrice and that Johnson girl.'

Half an hour later, after a gruelling struggle across what Bognor considered 'difficult terrain', they arrived at the Ghillies' Tomb.

'I was right,' called his companion, who, nimble as a goat, had gone on ahead. 'Here he is.'

Bognor, breathing very heavily by now, clambered up on to the rock alongside her, and looked down at the stream. There sitting on a large, smooth boulder, with his rod at his side was the McCrum. He was smoking a pipe and appeared deep in thought.

'Archie,' shouted Lady McCrum through cupped hands, 'Mr Bognor's arrived.'

The McCrum remained motionless and his wife called again.

'Cooeee,' she cried, the shrill sound reverberating around the narrow gorge. Still he didn't move. 'Come on,' she said to Bognor, 'we'll have to go closer.'

Finally, when they arrived, Sir Archibald

took the pipe out of his mouth and said, rattily, 'No need to shout, I heard you the first time. Morning, Bognor. Good journey I hope. I trust Mabel's been looking after you.' Then he returned the pipe to his mouth and went back to contemplating the waters.

Bognor began to say something, but before it actually came out, Lady McCrum put a finger to her mouth and shook her head at him. A minute passed in uneasy silence and then the McCrum stood up and jumped down from his perch. He was curiously dressed in thigh-length green waders, the McCrum kilt, a khaki anorak and a deer-stalker.

'Fish?' he asked Bognor.

'No, I'm afraid not.'

'Nothing to be afraid of. Shoot?'

'No.'

'Oh, Too bad. Never mind. Not a countryman, eh?'

'I suppose not.'

'Mmm,' the McCrum looked disapprovingly at Bognor's dress. 'Did I understand you were a relation of Humphrey Bognor's?'

'Distant, yes.'

'Oh. Good. First-class.'

They started to walk back to the castle, a return which Bognor found even more fatiguing than the outward journey. The Colonel said nothing about the purpose of Bognor's visit and confined his remarks to a few observations

178

about country matters. All that Bognor heard clearly was that he should read Nobbes' *The Complete Troller*, and always stick to a Durham Ranger or a Silver Doctor. He was too out of breath to make a coherent reply. When they arrived back at the castle, Sir Archibald said stiffly to his wife:

'Bognor and I have matters to discuss. We'll be in my den. Lunch at one?'

The McCrum's den was nothing that the comfortable womb-like word implied. It was the size of a large aeroplane hangar and about as draughty. Antlers and stags' heads festooned the panelled walls in a haphazard display and there were two glass cases of stuffed salmon. At the far end the window was of stained glass, on a religious theme.

'Used to be the chapel,' said the McCrum. 'Grandfather had a private chaplain. Father dispensed with him. Quite right in my opinion, I'm not a religious man myself. Don't hold with it except at Christmas and Easter, eh? You'll take a dram?'

He took a bottle and poured a large slug into two tumblers. It was very pale brown. 'Tallisker,' he said, 'Island malt. Know it?'

Bognor nodded. One of his tutors had had a liking, amounting almost to a fetish, for Tallisker malt whisky. It came from Skye.

'In that case you won't take water.'

Bognor would have preferred water but he

felt he had already done enough to antagonize his host.

'Well,' said the McCrum going to his desk and picking up a green file, 'when are they to be apprehended?'

'I don't honestly know,' he replied, 'I don't even know if they are going to be apprehended, but it's not my job. It will be done by the police.'

'I know the form, I know the form,' said the McCrum, rubbing his moustache and sitting down in a frayed brown leather armchair. 'Changed since my day. They'd probably have disappeared quietly then and no questions asked. Socialists changed all that sort of thing. Now. I've made some notes.'

'Notes?'

'Based on my observations of the guilty parties during my stay at Abney.' He preened his moustache and looked smug. 'I had my suspicions from the first. No idea they were going to resort to murder, but I had a pretty shrewd idea they were up to something. Right. Point one. Not to mince matters they were sleeping together.'

'I know that,' said Bognor, 'there's no law against it.'

'That's as may be. But I don't hold with it. I know it's considered very fashionable to carry on with a complete disregard for what I'd always been brought up to believe as decency and common sense, but I don't condone the behaviour of the farmyard. Particularly in someone of Grithbrice's pedigree. *And* she's black.' He stabbed a finger angrily in Bognor's direction. 'Black as your hat.'

Bognor resigned himself to a lecture.

'Two. Basil Lydeard told me she was a Mangolan. Poor old Lydeard couldn't tell a bleak from a gudgeon, but I knew at once what that meant. She was up to no good.

'Three. He was after Maidenhead and Abney's business. He and Abney'd got some harebrained scheme together. Approached me about it in a roundabout sort of way. Maidenhead told them what to do with it and so did I, but the Grithbrice fellow had his hooks into Abney, that much is certain.

'Four. And this will be news to you. Grithbrice tried to kill me that night we were playing that damn-fool game. No doubt about it. Luckily I know a thing or two about unarmed combat and I managed to fight him off until some help came. Still ricked my ankle badly, though.'

'You seem to have recovered very successfully.' The McCrum glanced across with an irritated expression and his cheek muscles twitched. He poured himself another Tallisker but offered none to Bognor.

'Five. Yes, well, naturally you know about these Mangolan claims. Now I've had

181

experience of these sort of people. I was in Burma with Wingate. I saw some of the things those Japanese did. And I saw something of the Mau Mau stink as well. These people don't pussyfoot around like you and your colleagues are doing. No messing about. Shoot first and talk later. Do you read Oliver Strange?'

'No.'

'You should. Might learn a thing or two.'

'I'm sorry,' said Bognor, 'but ...' The McCrum interrupted.

'Being sorry,' he said, 'is half your problem. No point in being sorry. It's always too late. I haven't finished. Now. The reason you're here today is because I spent yesterday creating a fuss. I've spoken to a good many people including some of your colleagues, and I'm bound to say that I find the situation most unsatisfactory.' He stood up and walked over to a particularly motheaten stag's head, staring it straight between the eyes. He then swung round in a gesture which Bognor reckoned he must have learnt in the Guards.

'So,' he barked in another Guards' mannerism, 'I have two things to say. One is that unless you have some good reason which you can now produce I shall expect an arrest. The second is that unless such an arrest is made within forty-eight hours of this moment I shall make a nuisance of myself the like of which has not been seen. Do I make myself clear?'

Bognor was stung, even though he knew that the man had to be placated.

'With the greatest possible respect, sir,' he said, trying hard, 'we have no proof.'

'I've given you all the damn proof you need.'

'Again with respect, sir, you have not. This is just theory.'

'Utter balls. I've never heard such nonsense.' He grabbed at the Tallisker and refilled his glass. 'Do you want me to ring your Minister immediately?'

'I'd rather you didn't, but if you insist. You see, sir, all you've given us so far are motives and in themselves they're not enough.'

'Balderdash. What about the claim from Algiers?'

'The Foreign Office are inclined not to believe it.'

'Sod the Foreign Office. Lot of pansies. He tried to kill me on the tennis court, didn't he?'

'So you say.'

'Are you doubting my word? No man alive doubts the word of a McCrum and gets away with it. Be very careful.'

'No, I wasn't doubting your word, sir, I'm only saying it isn't enough. We know there are enough motives to make us very suspicious of both Mr Grithbrice and Miss Johnson, but other people had motives too.'

'Such as?' The McCrum looked menacing. The Tallisker had not improved his temper and the twitch of his cheek muscles was pronounced. Bognor knew that it was unwise to say what he was about to, but he was unable to control himself. He did not like the way he was being treated and even in one as mild and subordinate as himself there were times when . . .

'You for one, sir.'

'I beg your pardon. I beg your pardon.' The McCrum's voice had risen several octaves and when he took two steps forwards it seemed to Bognor that physical violence was about to be offered. The moment passed and the Colonel had a fresh gulp of whisky. Bognor realized with further apprehension that it must be having some effect. On a long mahogany table in the middle of the room there was an old-fashioned Grundig tape recorder. The McCrum now paced over to it and started to play with it. He was obviously not good at machinery but after a few false starts he blew down the microphone and said in a contrived, official-sounding voice, 'Testing, testing, testing . . . the cat sat on the mat . . . now is the time for all good men to come to the aid of the party.' He pressed a switch and reversed the tape, then pressed again and stood back to listen. The voice which emerged from the machine bore only a passing resemblance to the McCrum's, but although partially muffled by crackling, the message could dimly be

184

discerned. 'The cat sat on the mat,' it reported, and 'Now is the time for all good men to come to the aid of the party.' Bognor took advantage of the interruption to steal another measure of Scotch from the rapidly emptying bottle of Tallisker.

'I was hoping,' the McCrum had executed his stiff military turn again, and was once more facing his guest, 'that there would be no need to have recourse to this machine. I had expected to be able to discuss this matter as one gentleman to another. That is evidently not possible. And if you are going to resort to cheap threats I would prefer to have them on the record should I wish to make use of them at a further time and date.' He puffed out his chest and stalked back to the machine. 'Would you mind,' he said, 'turning to face the recorder? I wish to have as clear a record as possible.' He then flicked the switch with a flourish and said into the microphone, enunciating very clearly, 'The following is a recording of a conversation between Colonel Sir Archibald McCrum of that ilk and Mr'—he looked over his shoulder—'What's your Christian name?' he asked.

'Simon,' said Bognor, with bad grace.

'And Mr Simon Bognor of, of, er ... Her Majesty's Government, which took place at McCrum Castle on Tuesday the 12th of May.' He glared at Bognor, and said, still enunciating

185

grotesquely, 'Now, sir, perhaps you would be so kind as to repeat what you have just said.'

'I only said,' said Bognor plaintively, 'that other people besides Anstruther Grithbrice and Honeysuckle Johnson had reason to dislike the Earl of Maidenhead.'

'Ho no, sir. Ho no, sir. You said more than that. A great deal more. You threatened me, sir. Threatened me. And I wish to have that threat recorded.'

Bognor swallowed. He was regretting his earlier remark. Not that he was worried any longer for his sake, or particularly scared of the McCrum, but in his present mood Sir Archibald was liable to do severe damage to the unfortunate Lady Mabel.

'I only meant that you had reason to dislike the Earl yourself.'

'Oh, come, sir, come, sir.' The McCrum was truculent and again Bognor lost patience.

'I mean, to be absolutely blunt,' Bognor realized he was shouting and dropped his voice, 'I mean that since you were being cuckolded by the Earl of Maidenhead, you had good reason, particularly given your extreme puritanism, to wish him dead.' There was silence. Sir Archibald turned off the Grundig. Bognor prayed inwardly for Lady McCrum's forgiveness. This was one way of finding out whether her husband knew, but hardly the one intended.

186

'Say that again,' he said, very quietly.

'I said you were being cuckolded by the Earl of Maidenhead. Your wife was his mistress. Look, honestly I didn't mean to interfere and it wasn't serious. It was just a little flirtation. Something to do with the change of life, I expect. I mean really there's no need to get steamed up about it.'

'Who in God's name told you this?'

Bognor was flustered. In such circumstances he invariably told the truth.

'Your wife did, sir. This morning.'

The McCrum said nothing. Very deliberately he picked up the internal telephone (an elderly Edwardian object) on his desk and wound it up. 'Mrs Campbell,' he said, 'please place Mr Bognor's belongings in the hall. He is leaving. There will be only two for lunch. No. A car will not be necessary. Mr Bognor will find his own way to the station.' He replaced the receiver.

'I have no more to say to you, sir,' he said, surprisingly evenly. 'You are, I trust, qualified for some other job, since I shall ensure you do not continue in this one. You will not be hearing further from me, but have every expectation that my solicitors will be in touch shortly. I must now ask you to leave forthwith.'

'Look, honestly,' Bognor was appalled at the thought of what would happen now. 'All right so I phrased it badly, but why don't you ask your wife? Get her to come down here and ask her.'

Once more the McCrum seemed to lose control for a moment. His cheeks twitched, his nostrils flared and he again took several steps towards Bognor, his sporran swinging aggressively and his hands bunched dangerously. Bognor did not give much for his chance in hand-to-hand combat. He stood his ground for a moment, watching mesmerized as the Scotsman advanced, then he turned and walked with as much dignity as was compatible with safety to the door. He reached it and continued down the stone-flagged corridor. As he walked he heard the McCrum's voice receding into the distance. 'Filthmonger ... coward ... don't think you'll get away with this,' then a jumble of words in which, abuse apart, he heard, 'Minister, slander and writ,' then the door slammed and there was merciful silence. He stopped and wondered which way to go. Eventually after wandering blindly along lengths of chill characterless passage he came out into the hall. Lady McCrum was standing there holding his overnight case in one hand and dabbing at her eyes with the handkerchief in the other.

'You ... you told him?' she said.

'I'm afraid so. He didn't seem to believe me.'

'I had an awful feeling he might not.'

'What did he say?'

'He just told me to leave immediately.'

'I know. Mrs Campbell told me. I've asked her to cut you some sandwiches quickly. I'd drive you in to Spean Bridge, but quite honestly I don't think I dare.'

'That's all right. It's very kind of you to bother about the sandwiches. I should be able to catch the night train to London.'

'It's a ten-mile walk.'

'Oh,' he smiled wanly. 'I'm awfully sorry,' he said feebly, 'I really did try.'

He felt very inadequate, and Lady McCrum was crying again.

'I suppose,' she said, 'if he didn't believe you, he won't say anything to me. Life will go on the same as before.'

'I don't know. He may have believed me. He just wasn't going to admit it. I'm sorry, I just don't feel I know him well enough to say.'

'But do you think he could have killed Freddie?'

'I got the impression he could have killed me, frankly. And I hadn't done anything, I just said something.' He saw the look of despair on Lady McCrum's face. 'I'm sorry,' he said, 'I ballsed it up, didn't I?'

There was a noise of shuffling slippers on stone and Mrs Campbell came in with a small package in greaseproof paper.

'The sandwiches, my lady,' she said surlily. She gave Bognor a look which suggested that she hoped they choked him, and shuffled off into the bowels of the castle. Then somewhere far away in the distance a door slammed, harsh steel-heeled feet banged along a corridor and they heard an angry alcoholic cough.

'You must go,' said Lady McCrum frantically. 'There's a sjambok on the wall in the library. He tried to use it on a man once. Thank you for trying. I'll write to you if anything happens or if there's anything I can do to help.' The footsteps' warning tattoo was approaching fast. He smiled feebly and hurried out of the door. 'I'm sorry,' he said as he left, 'please do write.'

Outside the rain had started again and the animals were howling an anguished chorus. He struggled on with the mac and slipped the sandwiches into the grip. Then he set his face into the north wind and started to walk.

CHAPTER NINE

Next morning he lay in the bath at the flat while Monica massaged his chest with Vick. 'And then,' he said, 'I had to walk all the way back in the rain. It was absolutely bloody. And that foul old woman had put spam in one sandwich and bloater paste in the other. And then when I got on the train all the sleepers had gone and there was no buffet. And a whole lot of drunken Scots got on at Edinburgh and sang all the way to York and then started being sick until Euston. Jesus Christ! The things I do for Parkinson.'

'Talking of Parkinson,' she said, 'he's been on twice this morning, asking if you were back.'

'Already?'

'I got the impression that he'd had several long harangues from your Scottish friend.'

Bognor pushed her away from his chest and wallowed. 'Any breakfast?' he asked.

'Eggs.'

'Scrambled eggs would be nice.' After she'd gone out to scramble, he lay back in the warmth of the soapy water and went over his performance once again. Whatever way he looked at it, and he looked at it from all the ways he could think of, the excursion had been a colossal personal disaster. He had gone to shut up the McCrum and had succeeded in making him not only generally angry, but personally vengeful too. Worse, he had no more idea whether the McCrum had realized that his wife was betraying him with Freddie Maidenhead. He groaned and looked at his feet. Each heel boasted a large blister and the soles ached. The nail of the little toe on his left foot was beginning to come away.

'Do you know,' he said when she returned, 'it was ten miles from the McCrums to the station?'

'Do you good,' she said, 'I've been thinking.

191

I think your friend was bluffing. I think he knew all about his wife and Maidenhead but he was so vain he didn't understand how anyone else could suspect. He realized Maidenhead might be indiscreet, but not Lady Mabel. It's other people knowing that will hurt him. Nothing else. It's just wounded pride.'

'Do you think he killed Maidenhead then?'

'If he claimed to be on the loo for all that time with *The Law o' the Lariat* and if he'd found out, then yes, I think he probably did. But I don't see why he'd kill Abney. Specially if he was impotent. Hang on, I must go and look at the eggs.'

Bognor got out of the bath reluctantly and looked apprehensively in the mirror. It was as bad as he feared. His eyes were bloodshot and puffy and his face looked blotchy. He put on a thick towelling dressing-gown, a present, like all his remotely respectable clothes, from Monica, and went in to the kitchen.

'I must go to work in a minute,' said Monica, ladling out eggs. Bognor could never keep track of her jobs. She hated to be tied down to anything in particular and therefore worked, when she felt like it or needed to, as a temporary secretary. 'But how about this for a theory? Suppose Lady McCrum was conning you. Suppose she never had an affair with Maidenhead. Suppose she imagined it.'

'Ridiculous.'

'Bad for you, though. Still, let's go a stage further. Suppose she was telling the truth. However she and her lover had a dreadful quarrel and when her husband disappeared to the loo with a book she took the opportunity to nip out and shoot her lover in the back. How about that?'

'Ridiculous too. I'm certain Lady McCrum was telling the whole truth. I feel very sorry for her.'

'You're just susceptible to sad middle-aged women.'

'Oh,' Bognor pushed his plate to one side, 'you're very good at scrambling eggs,' he said, 'but you're lousy at murder theories. I concede that either of the McCrums could have killed Maidenhead, but neither have any reason for doing in Abney. It has to be Green or Grithbrice. They're the only two who have a double motive.'

'Sure you aren't forgetting anyone?'

'Of course I'm forgetting people. We've got to find someone and those two are very good suspects. I've no intention of buggering the case against them with a lot of red herrings.'

'Like the McCrums, for instance?'

'Oh, go to work.' He smiled grudgingly. The affair was getting him down. He wished he could have stuck to arranging the security for official visits. He should have realized there'd be trouble when Parkinson first mentioned the

Umdaka of Mangolo. She kissed him and pushed the morning's *Times* at him.

'Stop thinking about it,' she said. 'Do the crossword or something. I'll see you this evening.'

'O.K.' Bognor sat down and turned to the back page. Despite every effort the problem wouldn't go away. He didn't even attempt the crossword for long. Instead he got dressed quickly and headed for the office. He might as well get this unpleasant interview over.

'Very well,' said Parkinson. 'Just tell me exactly what happened. In your own words. Slowly. I don't expect to believe it but I have to give you the benefit of some sort of doubt, and, in any case, if I'm going to fire you I'd better have your full account. For the files at least.'

'The *McCrum* said he'd have me fired.'

Parkinson looked thoughtful. 'I don't like that assumption of power,' he said, 'but I'm bound to say that if you said half what he claims, then he had every right to threaten you in every way he could think of.'

'I'll start at the beginning.'

'You'd better.'

Throughout the long story Bognor told, he was acutely conscious, not only of Parkinson's suspicious ferrety eyes, but also of the accusing gaze of Her Majesty the Queen behind him. As he spoke he was dimly aware that he was not making a very good impression. Even to him,

194

the story sounded thin, and his own part in it preposterous.

At last he came to a, literally, lame conclusion.

Parkinson was silent for a while and then he looked up and smiled. 'It has its funny side,' he said, 'and I sincerely doubt whether any other individual in the entire department would have handled it quite like you. *Could* have handled it quite like you, I should say.' He leant back and closed his eyes before continuing. 'Sir Archibald has telephoned me quite frequently since your precipitate departure. He was very angry and he was also very drunk. I didn't warm to him. However, what he said amounted to a charge of grossly improper and unprofessional conduct by one of my staff, whom I naturally had to defend. He didn't like that, by the way.'

Bognor shifted nervously. 'Thank you very much,' he said.

'Don't thank me,' Parkinson snapped. 'I had, unfortunately, no alternative. I happen to believe that any censure of my staff is a reflection on me. I was protecting myself.'

'Oh. I thought it was too good to be true,' said Bognor, who wondered if he was going to be sacked immediately, and whether he would be compensated for loss of earnings.

'What he told me, as far as I could understand it, was that you had upset the staff.

195

Subjected his wife to vicious and insensitive interrogation over kippers in the morning room, thereby reducing her to hysterics. That you then disturbed the fish in the river by your shouting and cavorting, and that finally you made "filthy" allegations, which he wouldn't repeat over the telephone and then threatened him. Oh and he said later on that you'd stolen some food.'

'I suppose that's a reference to the spam sandwich,' said Bognor.

'Look,' said Parkinson, 'I'm a forgiving sort of person but you try me, Bognor, you really do. However for the moment I will overlook the fact that you have made a potential irritant into a bloody menace and instead I will try to be positive. What do you think you achieved on this visit? *Achieved.*'

'I think the case against Cosmo Green has become rather, er ... compelling,' he said. 'And I think there are some reasons for suspecting McCrum.'

'Mmmm. I've been checking on your friend Sir Archibald, which is partly why I'm prepared to take a marginally less severe view of what happened. His friends and acquaintances have a remarkably uniform view of his character.' He picked up a piece of paper with scribbled notes on it. 'Autocratic ... cantankerous ... megalo-maniac ... bloody-minded ... difficult. I gather his military reputation was, shall we say, eccentric. Those whom I asked said that murder was definitely a possibility, but not except in the heat of the moment. In other words you were lucky to escape yourself, but he is unlikely to have accounted for Maidenhead. Still less for Canning. Premeditation is not his forte.'

'I see. So you're not prepared to entertain him as a suspect?'

'Everyone is guilty in my book until proved otherwise. You know that. But remember as well, there's only one motive and probably only two individuals who interest this department. Unless one or both these crimes were committed for political reasons we stay quiet. And the only political animals we have at the moment are Grithbrice and Johnson.'

'Any more news from Algiers?'

'The organization exists,' said Parkinson. 'Can't say much more than that. They're a motley lot. They could have made the claim to discredit Johnson. I gather, like most of these set-ups, they have their internal problems. However, Green. Green interests me.'

'I thought politcal motives were what interested you?'

'I'm interested in anyone who is trying to buy himself a parliamentary seat and access to what is laughingly called the Establishment. And besides, if he did it, then Grithbrice and Johnson didn't. Which is relevant.'

'So what do you want me to do now?'

'Continue to liaise wth the police. In the nicest, friendliest possible way. I don't want them on my back as well as McCrum. And have another word with Mr Green. Try confronting him with his misdemeanours. I fancy he'll react rather differently to McCrum. And as for that person, I suppose I shall have to tell him that you are to be disciplined.'

By the time he got to his own desk Bognor was dispirited. He still felt he was getting nowhere and he needed to try to get the puzzle back into a perspective which he felt it had scarcely ever had. He went back to his lists. What he wanted was someone who might chat away freely and who was also not under suspicion. He read through his notes. Only one person really fitted that category. Unless Isobel Abney wanted her husband out of the way, and all the evidence suggested she was merely sexually bored by him, there was no reason to think that she could have been involved in either crime. He decided to telephone and ask if he could take her to lunch.

'I'm sorry, sir, Lady Abney is not at home.' It was Mercer, the wartime special agent turned butler. No wonder, thought Bognor, he's so condescending, he'd probably have solved this by now. Unless he did it.

'I'm sorry,' he said, 'is that butlerese for she's there but doesn't want to talk to anyone? This is

198

Simon Bognor here.'

'I remember, Mr Bognor. No, Lady Abney is, as I say, not at home, and I mean precisely that. Would you care to speak to Mr Williams?'

'He'll have to do.'

'Very well, sir.'

There was a flurry of whirring and clicking before Peter Williams came on the line. From the strange echoing noise of his voice Bognor guessed he was using an amplifier. He wondered if there was anyone with him; or if the conversation was being recorded.

'Hello. Simon Bognor here. I wanted to talk to Lady Abney. Could you tell me where I could find her?'

'I'm sorry, old boy. She's left specific instructions she's not to be disturbed.'

'This is rather special. You know my interest.'

'Honestly, old boy, I'd tell you if I could, but it's more than my job's worth.'

Bognor swore under his breath. 'Surely,' he said, 'she was asked to keep in touch with the police?'

'Yes.'

'Well then?'

'Well, you're not police, are you, old boy. That's what you said.'

Again Bognor swore. 'So they'll have her address?'

'Of course.'

Bognor hung up and rang Smith.

'Funny you should mention it,' said Smith, 'I was going to have a word with you myself. It seemed a little peculiar. She's gone up to Hook.'

'Hook?'

'Staying with Cosmo Green.'

'Good God. First of all he's an appalling pouf, and secondly he may be a double murderer.' Bognor told him about the threats to Maidenhead, and Smith whistled softly.

'I think,' he said eventually, 'perhaps your boss is right. Better have a word with him.'

'Do you want to come?'

'No,' said Smith. 'Try to pretend you're the velvet glove concealing my iron fist. We don't want to frighten him overmuch. Not yet awhile.'

★　　★　　★

It took Bognor four hours to drive to Hook so that he didn't arrive until the afternoon. The estate was some six miles outside Hereford, past Stretton Sugwas on the Roman road. Unlike the other stately homes it was not open to the public all the time, but there were signposts none the less. Half a mile outside the village of Hook with its traditional black-and-white timbered houses and concomitant antique shops and tea shops he came to a lodge with a gate firmly closed. Barbed wire ran across it and along the adjoining walls. A large sign on the middle of the gate said, 'Hook House will be closed to the general public until the Whit Bank Holiday, when it will open throughout the holiday from 10 a.m. until 6 p.m.' Bognor was surprised. In the old days of Hook's former owners, the Dorsets, the house had been open most of the time, albeit on a chronically haphazard basis.

Gawain Dorset had been a contemporary of Bognor's at Oxford, and was now, he understood, commuting between his surviving estate in Caithness and a villa in Tuscany where he wrote doubtful verse. He had tried to keep Hook going after his father's death, but eventually the nudists and jazz bands with which he'd attempted to make the place pay proved too much for him. The final straw had been a gorilla which he'd purchased in a last desperate attempt to attract the coach trade and which had escaped and killed two pet dogs and a budgerigar before being shot by a local farmer for worrying sheep. After that they had sold to Mr Green, and, by the look of it, Mr Green was in the process of restoring some privacy to Hook.

Bognor got out of the Mini and walked up to the gate. Underneath the large notice there was a smaller one which said: 'All inquiries to Major Struthers, Estate Manager, the Dower House,

Hook.' Bognor had no intention whatever of entering into discussion with the Major. He banged on the gate. Nothing happened so he went back to the car and blew the horn. This time there was a response. A flap in the gate was opened and a voice said simply: 'Yeah?'

'I've come to see Mr Green.'

'Not here.'

'What do you mean?'

'What I say. Not here. Go away.'

Bognor didn't like the voice. It was whining. 'I insist on seeing him,' said Bognor, 'I'm a government inspector.'

'You'll have to see Major Struthers.'

'Oh come on.' Yet again Bognor was becoming irritated. 'Who are you? Let's have a look, I can't have a conversation with a hole in a gate.'

'Oh, all right.' A moment later the gate swung open to reveal a large fat man in the uniform of a security guard. He had a truncheon and an emaciated alsatian dog was attached to a chain on his belt. Bognor found the alsatian's silence unnerving. It sniffed at him. He showed the guard his identity card.

'Now,' he said, 'I haven't time to see Major Struthers. Is Mr Green really not here?'

'No.' The man was still surly, but apparently impressed.

'Where is he then?' The man remained silent and Bognor reluctantly produced a pound note

202

from his pocket. He was singularly inept at giving out bribes and hated doing it, but the guard didn't care about finesse.

'That all?'

Bognor peeled off another two. 'They left in the helicopter round lunch time.'

'They?'

'Mr Green and the lady.'

'Who was the lady? What did she look like?'

'About fifty. Hair going a bit grey. Not bad looking.'

'Thanks.' Bognor walked back to the car and accelerated away in a bad temper. In the village he went to a phone box and rang Smith.

'I know what you're going to say,' said Smith, immediately. 'He rang from the airport.'

'Saying what?'

'That they're going away for a few days to Green's villa in the south of Italy. Place called Maratea, about three hours south of Naples.'

'And you let them?'

'No alternative.'

'What flight were they on?'

'They weren't, Green has a BAC-111.'

'I suppose I just have to come back to London and wait.' He heard Smith laugh dryly. 'I've had a word with your Mr Parkinson,' he said, 'and we agreed it would do you good to have a day away from it all. You're on the ten o'clock flight to Naples. Tickets waiting at the Alitalia desk. You have a room booked in

203

Naples at the Hotel Mediterraneo, and a car to pick you up at seven-thirty in the morning and take you down to this place, Maratea. The driver will bring you back for the night flight home.'

'Last time I had a day away from it all,' said Bognor, 'I got blisters.'

CHAPTER TEN

It was a nerve-racking flight and the drive south from Naples was worse still. The autostrada was clogged with heavy lorries on their way to Reggio and Sicily beyond, and his driver weaved in and out of them as if he were driving a Ferrari and not a clapped-out old Fiat. Bognor was so nervous he hardly had time to take in the curve of the bay at Salerno, the luxuriance of the flowers, the charm of the hill-top villages.

'*Per favore*,' said Bognor haltingly as they cut out behind an articulated petrol lorry and into the path of an overtaking Maserati. 'A little slower, please.'

The driver, a crumpled middle-aged figure with his chauffeur's cap rakishly over one ear, turned round to face him. 'Bobby Charlton,' he said. 'You like Bobby Charlton. Is marvellous. I have been in England. Southampton.

Northampton. All over.'

Bognor sighed and held tightly on to the strap at his side. At Lagonegro they turned off the Autostrada on to a minor, windy, hilly road. This seemed a signal for the car to be driven even faster, but worse was to come after another dozen or so kilometres when they reached the coast and turned right. Here the road, which had room for only one car's width, followed the line of the cliff which rose higher and higher above the Gulf of Pollicastro. By the time they arrived in the village of Maratea the sweat had penetrated to his unsuitable tweed suit. At the centre of the village they stopped to ask the way of an elderly peasant with a donkey, who reacted immediately to the name of 'Signor Green'. There was a great deal of pointing and gesticulating before they set off again at the same suicidal speed.

Two miles out of the village after the road had moved inland they turned down a drive to the left. Two hundred yards down it they came to an automatic barrier and a young man in dark glasses and a lightweight suit emerged from the hut to one side and exchanged words with the driver. He peered in at Bognor and waved. The barrier was raised and they drove on.

Just as he feared they were about to plunge over the cliffside they emerged into a courtyard, surrounded on three sides by a futuristic bungaloid building. Bognor remembered his arrival at McCrum Castle. It had only been two days before. It seemed like an eternity.

As he stepped out of the car, part of the building slid to one side and a slim youth in dark blue trousers and white jacket with gold braid walked towards him and bowed slightly. He was, in a slightly feminine way, astonishingly good-looking.

'Good morning,' he said, with only a trace of accent. 'Signor Green is on the beach and asks if you would care to join him.'

Indoors Bognor just had time to notice the depth of the carpet, the efficiency of the air-conditioning, and the unequivocal obscenity of an original Picasso drawing in the hall, before he was descending to the level of the Mediterranean. It must have cost a small fortune, he reflected, just to cut a lift shaft through the rocks.

'Would you like to swim?' asked the young man, eyeing Bognor's tweeds with friendly disbelief.

'Yes, but I don't have any things.'

'I will arrange it.'

Bognor blinked as they re-entered daylight, then, shading his eyes, distinguished Cosmo Green standing a few yards away under a palm tree. He was wearing a vivid purple shirt and Bermuda shorts, and in his left hand he held a cocktail shaker.

'Simon, dear boy,' he shouted, waving the cocktail shaker in greeting, 'I'm glad you made it. Great to see you. Will you have a Bacardi?'

Bognor walked nervously across the mosaic tiles towards him, noticing that the palm tree had a fully equipped cocktail bar built round it. 'Isobel's in the pool,' said Mr Green, extending a fleshy hand. 'Or rather she's just out of it.' He pointed to the other end of the pool which was situated, superfluously Bognor thought, only a short distance from the inviting Mediterranean. Mr Green caught the look of disapproval.

'Very cold this time of year in the sea,' he said, 'too cold for comfort.' He finished shaking the Bacardi and released it into two frosted glasses on the bar. 'Very trim for her age,' he said, gazing towards Lady Abney who was standing by the diving board in a modest bikini. She was talking to a lithe young man in a minute white g-string. 'She likes Giovanni too, so that's nice,' said Mr Green sipping his drink. 'So,' he took Simon by the elbow, 'so, dear boy, I'm delighted to see you. What terrible clothes. We must get you into something more suitable. What can I do for you? It's a long way to come, to see us. We're very honoured.'

'I called at Hook,' said Bognor.

'So I heard,' said Mr Green tapping his nose. 'So I heard. That's why we were expecting you.' He stood back and looked at him. 'How long can you stay? You look terrible.'

207

'It's not really a social visit,' said Bognor, 'I'm here on business.'

'Business is always a pleasure to me,' said Mr Green. He pointed up to the cliff and beyond to a huge statue of Christ, arms akimbo. 'Biggest statue like that in the world, except for Rio.'

'I'm still investigating the murders at Abney,' said Bognor.

'Murders did you say? In the plural. You mean what happened to Canning and the captain was no accident? That's very bad indeed. Isobel wasn't very happy about it either. I told her not to be silly.'

Bognor found the Bacardi gave him renewed confidence.

'The point is,' he said, 'that you weren't being quite honest with me when you said that Maidenhead and Abney didn't owe you very much money.'

Mr Green laughed. 'Honesty never got anyone anywhere. So I told you a little white lie. So. Have another drink.'

Bognor accepted and Mr Green refilled his glass before continuing. 'So now I suppose you found out how much it was?'

'Yes.'

'Well,' he patted his paunch, 'it's not much to me. May have been more to them, but to me ...' He made an expansive gesture, encompassing the beach, the palm, the pool, Lady Abney and the villa at the summit of the cliff. 'What's two hundred thousand pounds?'

'Enough to buy you a peerage or membership of Pring's,' ventured Bognor, the alcohol spurring him on.

Mr Green laughed, a little too readily. 'I see you've been talking to someone,' he said. 'All right. I don't deny it. I lend my money, I want a return for it. I don't need more money, or if I need more money I invest in some shares or in some property or in some oil or something like that. But I say my money's as good as the next man's. All your so-called aristocrats bought their titles—or their ancestors did. That's what I'm doing. Buying a position for myself.'

'So,' said Bognor, 'you lent the money purely in order to buy yourself a position in what's laughingly known as Society.'

'Right in one, Simon,' said Mr Green, equanimity now apparently restored, 'I have money and no status. The English aristocracy have status and no money. So there is an opportunity to do good business.'

'But when Maidenhead and Abney wouldn't do what you wanted, you started to threaten them.'

'I what?' Mr Green seemed genuinely surprised. 'Now, Simon,' he said, 'I do hope for everyone's sake you haven't been listening to silly stories. In business, you understand . . . you understand business?'

'The basics.'

'In business if the guy you lend money to stops paying the interest you ask him nicely the first few times and then you say you're sorry you have to have the money back.'

'And if they haven't got the money?'

'The money is found,' said Mr Green, in a sinister fashion. Then he laughed. 'Me, I'm careful where I lend money. Remember I told you I would never lend money to that old Lydeard? Never get it back that's for why.'

'But Abney wouldn't get you into Pring's and Maidenhead wouldn't get you a peerage.'

'So I was asking nicely. I always asked nicely.'

'No threats?'

'No threats. And even if I had threatened them, which I wouldn't, where are the witnesses I ask myself? Anyway what are you saying? That I killed the golden geese because the eggs were late? You have to be joking. I should be so silly. All right, so I need my status, so with this I can afford to wait.'

'What about Lady Abney? How long's this been going on?'

Mr Green looked up-pool for a moment, and waved in her direction. She waved back and blew a kiss. 'I'm sorry, Simon. How long has what been going on?'

'Well, you and Lady Abney, of course.'

Mr Green looked at Simon through narrowed eyes and then reached inside his purple shirt and scratched his chest. He had a hairy chest and the hair, which was turning silver, sprouted out of the top of the shirt towards his chin.

'If you didn't have a nice open English face, Simon,' he said, 'I might think you were a very cynical person. Now look up there,' and he pointed again to the other end of the pool where Lady Abney was lying watching as the boy in the white g-string did cartwheels. 'Now there you see one English lady. She is more than fifty years old. All right, so she is well preserved but she is still more than fifty years old. Her husband has just died, in a nasty mess. She is very sad. The press are chasing her. You also see one young Italian boy. He is exquisite. You look back here at me and what do you see? You see a fat, rich, middle-aged Jew who prefers to sleep with beautiful boys than women of more than fifty. And something else. English ladies, even when they are more than fifty, don't sleep with people like me. You perhaps. Though I understand Lady Isobel thought you less than passionate the night you were pushed in the river.'

He laughed and winked. Simon, who had forgotten the incident, choked on his drink and blushed. 'Don't look so sad. Self-knowledge is a wonderful thing. We have a saying in Yiddish, "Truth is the safest lie." Very true saying. Now you want a swim? Here is Sandro with your bathing things.' He laughed again. 'Don't look so nervous. He only shows you where to change. He won't touch you. Not unless you ask.'

Bognor blushed. Mr Green had read his thoughts precisely. He allowed himself to be led off to a changing room which instead of the usual minute cubicle, was a spacious air-conditioned room with a daybed, a dressing-table equipped with scents and colognes and a fridge of cold drinks.

'The sauna is through here,' said Sandro opening a door at the back. Bognor thanked him and locked the door after he'd left. Then he changed into the mercifully baggy and British trunks which had been provided. He didn't see himself in a silver g-string.

Outside he felt pudgy and white. Gingerly he eased himself into the pool, realizing when he was halfway in that the water was almost warm. Mr Green came to the edge, and looked at him with approval. 'Good boy,' he said, 'much better. Have a good refreshing swim, and then you'll be ready for another drink. But,' he struggled down on to his haunches and whispered, 'I know you have to talk to Isobel, but try to be careful. She may not look upset, but remember looks can be deceptive., Take me, for example.' He laughed. 'Her father was the Earl of Ormskirk. You like seafood?'

'Yes,' said Bognor. He pushed off into the tepid water and began to swim in a slow meticulous breaststroke. It was, he knew, not an elegant performance but it got him where he wanted. Rather like his approach to life in general. At the other end of the pool he climbed up the steps, puffing heavily. To his surprise a small boy in overalls was waiting with a tray and a towel on which there was another glass of Bacardi. He took both and walked over to where Lady Abney was still watching the g-stringed catamite doing PT.

'Simon,' she said, standing up and removing her dark glasses. At her age she shouldn't really have worn the bikini and her skin had a slightly wrinkled appearance round the navel and the upper chest, but she had the shape for it. 'How delightful.' They shook hands. 'This is Giovanni,' she said, waving in the direction of g-string who was standing on his head. 'He speaks absolutely no English whatever, poor darling.' Giovanni somersaulted back to an upright postion and smiled sexily. Bognor smiled back awkwardly.

'I know, Simon. You can help us,' she said, sitting down on the edge of a convenient hammock. 'Cosmo and I couldn't work this out at all. It's the answer to a riddle and we can't think what the question can have been. "One rode a horse and the other rhododendron." Now what can that be the answer to?'

Bognor drank white rum and wondered why everything was so confusing.

'I'm not awfully good at riddles. I'm sorry about the will.'

For a moment she looked as if the façade of brittle gaiety might collapse, but only for a moment. 'Yes,' she said, 'but there's really no need. Canning and I had discussed it and it made perfectly good sense. Quite honestly I'm not crazy about Abney, and I'm rather like poor old Basil Lydeard. I'm not sure I like all those people traipsing around looking at you. As for money, I have a little of my own. And Canning had the most enormous life insurance policies made out in my name. I'm really not too hard done by and there are always friends like Cosmo to help out. The only aspect I do rather regret is Tony Grithbrice getting it. I have to confess that young Master Grithbrice is not my favourite person.'

An ignoble thought occurred to Bognor. Perhaps Lady Abney had killed her husband for the insurance? In conjunction with Cosmo Green who was maddened by Abney's refusal to put him up for Pring's?

'I went to see Cumberledge,' he said.

'Oh, he's ghastly,' she said, 'dry as a stick but wet with it. I don't know how he manages it. I suppose he talked about sex?'

'As a matter of fact, yes.'

Lady Abney arched her eyebrows. 'Typical. It's why I changed. What did he tell you? That I was sleeping with Cosmo?'

214

'No.'

'But I suppose he said I was sleeping with half Burke's. Well that's no particular secret though I do think it's extremely indelicate of Cumberledge to discuss it with a perfect stranger. I mean, I do like you enormously, Simon, and so did poor dear Canning. But we haven't known each other very long.'

'Cumberledge did say something about Mr Green having threatened your husband over some money.'

She frowned for a moment, as if she was trying to remember. 'Oh Cosmo and Pring's. Poor Cosmo. He is a poppet. Really, in his curious Levantine way he is the sweetest of people, but he is incorrigibly vain. Canning and I shrieked with laughter about Pring's, but I don't think Cosmo was really serious. He wouldn't know what to do once he got into Pring's, *and* he wouldn't know anyone, *and* even if he did they'd all cut him. It's too absurd.' She pronounced the 's' of absurd as if it was a 'z'. Bognor, on his third rum, found it rather attractive.

'Cumberledge thought your husband took it seriously.'

'Oh, Cumberledge is a fossilized old woman. He's been reading too much romantic fiction. I'm sure he gave you the impression that Canning and I were fearful enemies.'

'Not quite.'

'But almost. Canning and I remained the best of friends all our lives. There was just one area where our interests ceased to coincide. That was very upsetting at first, I don't deny it, but later we came to an arrangement. It's what we call being civilized and it worked very well. Cumberledge is too concerned to force people into court so that he can get his fee. That automatically makes things uncivilized and acrimonious. It was one thing I made Canning promise. Never anything legal, and especially never through Cumberledge.' She paused. 'You know, I have a vague feeling you don't wildly enjoy being a whatever you are.'

Bognor shrugged. 'I don't mind the ordinary work but I'm not crazy about murders. This is only the second lot I've done.'

She smiled. 'Oh dear, we are being serious, aren't we?' She stood up and stretched her long, still-elegant legs. 'Let's go and freshen our drinks a little and then we'll solve your crime over lunch. Only, so that none of us get over-excited about it, let's try to think of it all as a puzzle. Like the question to "who rode a horse and who rhododendron". That way it might even be rather fun. After all, we can't bring them back, can we? And I'm sure they'd both want us to enjoy catching the villain.'

They walked back to Green's palm tree, slowly. The Mediterranean sparkled in the sun and away near the horizon they heard the distant hum of a small motor-boat dragging a water skier behind it. It was very still and quite hot. 'Getting near siesta time,' she said. 'When do you have to leave?'

'I'm booked on the night flight home.'

'How sad. It would do you good to lose some of that terrible London pallor.'

'Yes.' He would have liked it and for a moment he was almost tempted to send Parkinson a cable saying, 'Must keep alongside prime suspect. Returning later' but he rejected the thought as soon as it occurred. Instead he realized that he would have to change back into his hairy tweeds for lunch.

'We've found you some more suitable clothes,' said Green, when they reached his tree. He was sitting under it and had mysteriously acquired a parrot to which he was feeding nuts and muttering goodnaturedly. 'Sandro will show you. I hope they're better than the ones you had after you fell in the river.' He laughed at the thought and both Bognor and Lady Abney joined in. 'We'll see you upstairs when you've changed,' he said.

Bognor rejoined them, wearing an Italian linen suit in cream, with a lilac shirt and dark blue rope-soled sneakers. He felt cooler and the clothes, though inappropriate to himself, were much more appropriate to his surroundings. They also fitted. Green still wore the Bermuda shorts and the purple shirt; Isobel Abney had

217

changed into heavy wooden sandals and a curious silk kimono. They were sitting on a vine-covered terrace, looking out to sea. On the round wicker table there was a heavy stone flask dripping with condensation, and three silver goblets. As Bognor sat down at the third place three servants entered with an extraordinary assortment of Mediterranean crustaceans, squid, octopi, red mullet and innumerable unidentified marine objects.

'Isobel says we're going to play detectives, which is all right by me if it helps you to put things in order.' Cosmo waited while one of the boys poured out the wine. 'You'll like this,' he said, 'it's very special, made by some good friends of mine from down south. Business friends, you understand,' he added.

Simon watched as the servants heaped more and more seafood on to his plate. When they'd done, he said, 'My only rule is absolute truth.'

'We have to pretend that both Freddie's and Canning's death were murders,' said Lady Isobel.

'Pretend?' asked Bognor.

'Accept,' said Mr Green. 'Simon, you begin.'

Bognor started to break into a lobster. 'The only two who almost certainly didn't shoot Lord Maidenhead are the two who spent the night at the Compleat Angler. If they had they would have been spotted by the hotel staff and we've checked that out—or the police have—they were there all night. Otherwise no one has an alibi except that they were in bed with a partner. That isn't an alibi, that's conspiracy.'

Lady Abney remarked on the excellence of the wine. 'I happen to know it couldn't have been my husband,' she said, 'but I suppose you won't accept that.'

'Keep it at the back of our minds,' said Green. 'Nobody except me and Lady McCrum much liked Freddie. So count us out for the moment.'

'No,' said Bognor. 'You weren't getting the interest on your loan to him. And she could have had a tiff with him.'

'Have it your way, my boy. McCrum is jealous of Freddie's seducing his wife. Miss Johnson wants him dead on account of some political deal I don't understand. Grithbrice wants him dead to please his friend *and* because Maidenhead is a difficult rival who won't be bought.'

'He *was* difficult to buy, wasn't he?' said Bognor.

'No unpleasantness, Simon,' said Cosmo sharply, 'otherwise we can't help.'

'Sorry,' said Bognor, stuffing himself with squid. 'This is fantastic.'

'I like simple things,' said Mr Green. 'Isobel, you had no reason to kill Freddie.'

'I didn't care for him, but not enough to kill

219

him,' she said.

'That leaves one,' said Green. 'Nice old Basil Lydeard. Anyone think of any reason why he would kill Freddie?'

'No,' they chorused.

'Right,' said Green, 'let's remember that. Now Sir Canning.'

'The most obvious suspect is the main beneficiary in the will,' said Bognor, 'who would be helped by his black girl friend as a reward for previous services.'

'I suppose,' said Lady Isobel, 'we have to consider the two who spent the night at the Compleat Angler. I must say I thought that was incredibly poor form. That woman really does let the side down.'

'Not for the moment,' said Green. 'They complicate matters. The McCrums have no motives this time?' He looked round the table and the other two shook their heads. 'And neither of us.'

Again Bognor remonstrated. He mentioned the life insurance, trying to make a joke of it and reminded them of Cumberledge's evidence.

After some griping they agreed 'for the sake of the game' to concede motives. 'So,' said Green, 'that leaves us with Basil Lydeard. Does he have a motive?'

Again, less happily this time, they all said 'no'. The servants came in again to clear away the fish. 'Now, Simon,' said Mr Green, 'I have my figure to watch. I'll have some grapes and maybe some dolcelatte, but you have something else. Anything. Anything, eh, Carlo?'

'Si, Signor Green,' said the senior boy. Bognor wondered if they were a harem, and said he'd be happy with cheese.

'Let's think about the nice old Marquis from Somerset,' said Isobel, 'and talk about something more cheerful until we've finished.'

For the next twenty minutes they discussed servants and money and how Mr Green was going to introduce Bognor to some friends so that he could make enough of one to be able to afford the other. Finally when lunch had been cleared away they went back to the pool and sat by the edge with their feet dangling in the water. A boy brought three glasses and a bottle of Sambucca Negro. Cosmo Green watched him pour it out and then applied a light to the top of each one with the flame from his heavily jewelled lighter. Bognor watched the three little blue flames and thought of Basil Lydeard.

'A funny thing happened to me and the Marquis,' he said finally, 'on the day Sir Canning died.' He told the story of Basil Lydeard and the interlopers and the poker.

'I think that's rather significant,' said Isobel Abney, when he'd finished.

'Oh. Why?' he asked.

She blew out her drink, and frowned. 'In all the years I've known him I've never ever seen him lose his temper like that. You saw him during the tennis. Everyone else was furious, but he just seemed mildly put upon.'

'My feeling,' said Green, holding his flame up to the sky and inspecting it, as if he were examining the watermark on a banknote, 'is that behind that nice gentle shell there was a lot of very angry person bubbling away.'

'I thought that was his liver playing up,' said Bognor facetiously.

'No. More than liver,' said Green. 'When you've been around as long as I have you start to notice things other people don't see. The first thing I thought to myself when I met the old man was, Cosmo, this old aristocrat is all twisted up inside.'

'Oh, Cosmo, you didn't. You've always thought the same as I do. He's just a nice harmless old buffer.'

'Nice harmless old buffer on the outside maybe. But nice harmless old buffers don't threaten innocent members of the public with pokers.'

'But they weren't innocent. They were trespassing.'

'Did you really never see him lose his temper?' asked Bognor.

Lady Abney made gentle splashing movements with her feet. 'I honestly don't think so.' She went on splashing idly. 'No, wait a moment, that's not quite true. Years ago we

222

went down for the first of his annual traction engine dos and it absolutely poured with rain. It came down in buckets and buckets and buckets all the night before and all that morning and hardly anyone came and his own engine got stuck in the mud. He lost his temper then. It was terribly funny if it hadn't been so pathetic. He got down from the cab and stood in front of it shouting at it as if it was a horse. He used the most appalling language. In the end Dorothy had to take him away and make him lie down. Poor old Dot.'

'Dorothy?' asked Bognor and then paused. 'Did you say traction engines?'

'Yes,' said Lady Abney, 'Dot's the Marchioness. She's a dear. Very countrified and absolutely hates going away. That's why she wasn't at Abney last weekend. Yes, traction engines, why?'

'Did he drive one himself?'

'He tried. Without much success, like most of the things he tries.'

'And he has an annual traction engine festival?'

'He did. For about three years, but it never worked. No one was interested, so he gave it up and bought the bison instead.'

'Forgive my ignorance,' said Cosmo who had been looking uncharacteristically puzzled. 'But would someone tell me what is a traction engine?'

'From the Latin *trahere* to draw,' said Bognor, 'an engine which pulls things.'

'So I don't have the benefit of your education,' he said testily. 'So what's so special about these ones?'

'What's special,' said Bognor, suppressing his excitement badly, 'is that these traction engines are powered by steam. And perhaps you remember that during lunch that day our friend from Somerset asked if he could have a glance at the *Lysander* before the official opening. Then later when the police asked him about it he said he didn't know anything about steam engines. Obviously nobody remembered his obscure traction engine exhibition because no one much went to it and it stopped years ago. Anyway, as you said, he's such an old buffer nobody bothered to take him seriously.'

'So,' said Mr Green, 'you have a practical possibility that he could have interfered with the steam engine in the boat.'

'I think so,' said Bognor.

'But that doesn't prove anything,' said Lady Isobel. 'You know that any of you could have sneaked a look at the boat beforehand without any trouble. And you haven't given the old thing a proper motive. Why should he want to kill them both? Grithbrice has a motive for both of them.'

'I'm not so sure,' said Mr Green. 'I think perhaps the boy has hold of something

224

interesting. Now am I right that our Somerset friend is a very conservative old gentleman? He likes his hunting and shooting and fishing. Now he's older than everybody else. He can't adapt to change so quickly. He inherited the house late. He hates people he doesn't know paying to come to look at him.'

'We all hate that, Cosmo, surely, but we don't go round killing people because of it.'

'He would have beaten a whole family to death with a poker.'

'That's an exaggeration.'

'But why kill Freddie and Canning?'

'Because they were the ones who were forcing the pace. They made him commercialize and pay money to go to conferences and buy bloody bison and sell his Canalettos and change everything. And finally it got too much for him and he decided to stop them. He thought that if he got rid of the show business peers then he could stop having to be in show business himself.'

'That's not logical.'

'It's logical enough for someone who's going slowly batty.'

They all stopped at once. One of the boys approached and poured more Sambucca, which Green lit once more. The sun and the drink and the excitement were making Bognor sleepy. He yawned. 'It's all speculation in the end,' he said. 'Impossible to prove.'

225

'And,' said Green, 'no jury will believe a motive like that one. Whereas any jury will believe Grithbrice's motive. Once twelve Englishmen hear that the Grithbrice boy was due to inherit that estate they won't hesitate about waiting for evidence.'

'And,' added Isobel Abney, 'once they see his girl friend they'll be certain he killed Freddie too.'

Bognor looked at his watch. 'If I'm going to get my plane I'll have to go in a minute.'

'Right,' said Mr Green. 'Let's finish the game. Everyone write down on a piece of paper who they think did the murders. No, wait.' He pondered a moment and then clapped his hands. A boy came running. 'Giuseppe,' he said, 'fetch three typewriters and three sheets of paper.'

They waited in silence until boys returned with three small tables and three electric typewriters on very long leads.

'Now,' said Mr Green. 'We all type the name of our guilty person on the paper and fold it up. All the typefaces are the same so we won't know who suspects who. So. Ready. Off we go.'

When they had finished a boy was summoned to shuffle the pieces of paper and read them out.

'Anstruther Grithbrice,' he read first, murdering the name so that it was barely comprehensible. The second was Grithbrice again. The third, however, was Lydeard.

226

'You know something,' said Green, when the boy had been dismissed. 'Whichever one it is, I think he's going to do it again. And the very interesting thing is that he's going to kill the other.'

Bognor and Lady Abney looked at him uncomprehendingly. 'How do you work that out?' asked Bognor.

Mr Green tapped his nose. 'Grey matter,' he said, 'grey matter. If Grithbrice is killing people he is killing them so he can make his business empire bigger still, is that right?'

They nodded.

'He killed Freddie Maidenhead because he wouldn't join the business and because his girl friend wanted him dead for political reasons. He killed Canning for the estate. Next he'll kill Lydeard because the old man won't join his business and because Lydeard has more potential than any stately home in Britain. Except Hook and, so help me, Hook stays private.'

'He might try to kill you,' said Bognor, obviously.

'He should be so lucky,' said Mr Green contemptuously. 'You look at my security. Tony Grithbrice has no chance of killing me. Now,' he continued, 'if Lydeard is doing the killing he is doing it to stop his life being made a circus. Am I right?'

Again they nodded.

227

'So who, now, is going to be the big stately home circus man? Who runs the big top now? Eh? Mr Grithbrice! Abney-Arborfield Enterprises. Am I right?'

They all had a feeling he was right. Sandro appeared that moment with a suitcase. 'I have brought Mr Bognor's tweed suit,' he said. 'It has been cleaned and pressed as you asked, sir.'

Bognor started to protest but Green would hear none of it.

'You keep the clothes,' he said. 'Nobody else can wear them.'

It was time to go. With some reluctance Bognor looked round once more at the palm tree bar and the twinkling water and said good-bye. In a few minutes he had gone up in the high-speed lift, out past the Picasso, and was sitting anguished in the back of the car as it negotiated the zigzag bends of the switchback cliff road. From the alcoholic fumes which came wafting towards him on wings of garlic he recognized that the return journey was going to be as alarming as its predecessor. He shut his eyes and tried to banish reality with sleep.

CHAPTER ELEVEN

By the time he got back to the office he was shattered. He had only managed a few hours' broken sleep because Monica had insisted on going over every detail of his outing and also, with no regard for his exhaustion, on sex. She thought he had allowed himself to be soft soaped by the two of them and decided that the whole affair had been plotted by Green and Lady Abney, who were, despite the army of lissom Italian youths, lovers. Sitting in front of the Queen and Parkinson at eight-thirty, he scarcely knew what to think, let alone say.

'Hunches, hunches, it's nothing but bloody hunches and ifs and buts and on the one hands and hypothetically speakings,' said Parkinson angrily, 'I send you to bloody Naples and all you find out is that the Marquis of Lydeard once owned a traction engine which is something you could have found out a great deal more easily and a great deal more cheaply, and, I might add, a great deal less enjoyably, by looking in the library of the *Western Gazette* in Taunton or even by talking to the unfortunate Marquis himself. Instead of which you go gallivanting off to the Mediterranean and allow yourself to be lulled into a state of gullibility by this fat Jewish crook and his mistress.'

'She's not his mistress, he's as queer as a coot.'

'One of the many troubles with you, Bognor, is that you're so bloody naïve. What makes you so certain he's queer?'

Bognor told him and Parkinson dismissed it

immediately as lascivious speculation. He banged the table. 'I want facts,' he said repeatedly. At last when he had recovered, he said, quite calmly, 'I am afraid I'm now going to have to do something I should have done a long time ago. Take you off this assignment and suspend you pending a decision. I just can't take much more.'

Bognor sucked his teeth. He had been half expecting something like this and decided to take a risk. 'Will you give me one more chance?'

'No. You've had dozens of one more chances. No more.'

'It will take less than five minutes.'

'What is it?'

Bognor told him and made as if to leave, but Parkinson pushed the telephone across the desk to him.

'Do it here. I want to hear it direct from him. No cheating.'

Bognor dialled Smith's number. 'Hello,' he said. 'Listen, don't ask me any questions. This is vital, can you tell us exactly where Grithbrice and Lydeard are?'

There was a pause before Smith replied. Then he said, 'You're on to something, aren't you? I only heard this morning. Grithbrice is spending a couple of days with the Lydeards in Somerset.'

'Aha,' said Bognor triumphantly. 'Would you

mind repeating that to my superior who is sitting opposite.' He passed the receiver across to Parkinson and silently congratulated Cosmo Green. Green had been right. That was the only explanation. There would be a third murder any time now. The only question remaining was who would murder whom. He was lost in this speculation when he realized that Parkinson was talking to him again.

'You win, Bognor,' he said, 'but this really is the last time. You have until noon tomorrow.'

'What do you want me to do?' he asked, and was rewarded with a flat resigned stare and a shrug.

'Make the most of your last few hours,' he said. 'Do what you bloody like. Just stay away from me.'

Bognor returned to his desk, elated. Adrenalin was beginning to flow and he felt a sense of challenge and of impending solution. The murderer was going to reveal himself at Lydeard within hours. Of that he was now certain, though he recognized, with a twinge of doubt, that his intuition was notoriously fickle. He hummed a few bars of Handel and went to the library for the Lydeard number, returned, dialled, and spoke to the Marquis.

'Aha,' said the Marquis. 'Expect you want to come and have a bit of a jaw with the Grithbrice bounder and his floozie.'

'That's right,' Bognor recognized that this

231

was a useful passport to an invitation.

'Sound thinking. Good place to get the truth out of him down here. We're very quiet. You can use the library. Look forward to seeing you. Driving down? Good. I'll tell Dot to have a bed made up.'

★   ★   ★

Unlike Abney House and McCrum Castle there was nothing Victorian about Lydeard. The 'New building' was a cloistered courtyard to the rear, which was the work of James Wyatt at the end of the eighteenth century. Since then no Lydeard had had the cash or the inclination to add further. Bognor arrived in the watery sun of the afternoon, driving slowly through the park behind a coach from Shepton Mallet, which appeared to contain a Women's Institute. The sky was cloudless, and so pale that it might have come from one of the Canalettos for which the place was famous. To the north, the red and green checks of the Quantock hills faded into woodland and then bare grass, gorse and heather at their summits. All around the winding drive there were vast oaks and elms sloping away to a reedy lake, built, not by Capability Brown as one might have expected, but by a Marquis of Lydeard who had been at landscape gardening while Brown was still a child.

Bognor changed down a gear as the Women's Institute slowed to 5 m.p.h., gazing west to the great maze of Lydeard, rivalled in Britain only by Hampton Court and, in modern times, perhaps, by Michael Ayrton's creation for Mr Armand G. Erpf in the Catskill mountains. Then a further bend in the drive, a rattle over a cattle grid which crossed the ha-ha, separating park from formal garden and they could see the house. It was his first visit and he was entranced. It had, he conceded, none of the formal correctness of most of the French chateaux, but a rambling unity instead. Almost every century and every Lydeard had added a little, even if it was only a door or a window, and the resulting meld was a family history in brick, stone and mortar. Any cracks were papered over with jasmine and honeysuckle and climbing roses and a huge purple wistaria which, Bognor dimly recalled, was claimed as the oldest in England. Under this foliage the house showed a grey yellow for the stone, and a mellow red Somerset brick for the eighteenth- and seventeenth-century portions.

It lacked ostentation, but three kings of England had visited here and Monmouth, on his way to the disaster of Sedgemoor, had slept in the great bedroom. Later Judge Jeffreys had returned and hanged one John Lydeard and forty of his men from gibbets at the lodge gates. Cromwell had taken it earlier and many many years later it had been used in the Second World War for a purpose which even now was not disclosed. Peter Lydeard, the hero of the Elizabethan House of Commons, and Raleigh's friend, Sir Percy Lydeard, Aylmer Lydeard, the Romantic poet; Gertrude Lydeard, reputed mistress both of Palmerston and Prince Albert, and Arthur Lydeard, the penal reformer, had all been born and lived here, along with the innumerable Lydeards who had fought in England's wars and administered England's colonies or who, more often than not, had sat in Somerset and watched the cider apples grow.

The coach from Shepton Mallet turned down a track to the coach park, which was in full view of the house and on lawn which previous parkers had turned red-brown with their slipping tyres. An ice-cream tent flapped gently in the breeze and effectively ruined the sublime view of the park and lake; and a new pine structure, which said 'Drivers' on the door, blocked off the view of the west front. A signpost, the only one Bognor could see, directed the public to bison, lavatories, house and picture gallery in four completely different typefaces and the gardens seemed to be totally covered with a thin film of litter. It seemed, to Bognor, a high price to pay for the privilege of living at Lydeard and with a little shiver he wondered if, in a similar position, he too might be driven to murder.

me.' Another shot bore testimony to the accuracy of this claim and was followed by: 'Come on out and take it like a man you nigger-loving little pimp. Thought you'd pulled the wool over my eyes did you? You'd have drowned by now if that fat man from the Ministry hadn't saved you. Coward.'

Bognor crawled alongside Grithbrice and started to tie a handkerchief round his arm. It was a rough-and-ready job but it stopped the worst of the bleeding. Then he took hold of the gun. It was a twelve-bore. 'I'm a lousy shot,' he said, 'but it should be enough to scare him off. Cartridges?' Grithbrice began to use his good arm to open his breast pocket, while Bognor peered out from behind the tree.

'Hurry,' he said. 'He's almost reloaded and he's coming closer.' Before Bognor could put two catridges in, Lydeard shot twice more. From the amount of tree he was removing each time it was quite clear that he was getting much too close for safety. And since, it now seemed, he'd tried to murder Bognor too, his safety was as unsure as Grithbrice's.

Bognor looked apprehensively at the twelve-bore in his hands. He had only previously shot at clay pigeons; never at anything living, and certainly never at people. He would naturally try to miss the Marquis though he couldn't be sure he would succeed and he had better hurry. 'Oh, God,' he said out

267

loud, 'here goes.' He stood up, pressed the weapon into his shoulder, pointed it high and peered round the corner of the tree. The Marquis who was no more than twenty-five yards away was slowly reloading. He looked purple and his hands appeared to be shaking. Bognor realized that his, too, were quivering more than usual. With great deliberation he took aim at a point some three feet above Lydeard's head and fired. The explosion knocked him two steps backwards and when he staggered back to see what effect it had had, he saw that Lydeard was standing in the same place with his gun loaded.

'Bastard,' shouted the Marquis. 'And no better shot than your bloody father. Come on out!'

Bognor shrugged, and wondered if he should fire the other barrel. Then he decided to try a touch of the strong arm of the law. Holding the gun at his hip and pointing it at Lydeard he moved out from behind the tree and confronted him.

'It wasn't Grithbrice, it was me,' he said. 'Now put that gun down before you do anything you regret. This is loaded and I may have to fire. Put your gun down now and I'll do what I can with the police. But come along now, and for God's sake be sensible.'

Just for a moment he thought it had worked. Basil Lydeard stood stock still staring at Bognor and his shotgun. His mouth started to open and he seemed on the point of speech. Then, without warning, he dropped his gun, swung round and charged off into the undergrowth, shouting, 'Help, help, murder.'

'Bugger,' said Bognor angrily, and released the remaining barrel in the vague direction of the fleeing peer. It missed by a mile. 'Come on,' he shouted at Grithbrice. 'After him.'

'Can't,' moaned Grithbrice, holding his hand. 'I've been hit. You go.'

Bognor grabbed him by his good arm. 'No,' he said. 'Both of us. I want a witness. Come on. Hurry.' Together they set off on their pursuit, Bognor spurred on by adrenalin and excitement, half dragging Grithbrice through the wood.

Ahead of them they could hear the Marquis crashing through the foliage, still shouting 'Help' and 'Murder' for all he was worth. His dogs had fled with him and kept up an incessant baying. Bognor and his injured companion didn't know the area and Grithbrice, apart from being in a state of shock had also lost a lot of blood. They floundered along in Lydeard's wake, but it was clear that they were losing ground and they were still well away from the road when they heard a car door slam and the wheeze of an ancient self-starter which quickly gave way to an angry roar, as the Marquis revved the engine of the Lagonda. A second later there was a skidding sound and the car could be heard roaring away down the road in the direction of Crowcombe and Minehead.

'Hurry,' screamed Bognor, still heaving Grithbrice through the wood. 'We must get him.' Grithbrice responded in an incoherent daze. He was very white but when they got to the Mini they were only a minute or two behind the Lagonda. Bognor strapped them both in and drove off.

'Hold tight,' he shouted. 'I'm not used to this sort of thing. Anything may happen.' Luckily, he realized, the Lagonda's superior speed was unlikely to tell as the road was narrow and twisting. Anyone taking these corners at much more than 60 m.p.h. would be in the ditch in no time. He pushed the car to about that speed and started to skid towards Crowcombe. Most of the time he was on the wrong side of the road and more than once they brushed the hedgerow, but apart from a near miss with a tractor the journey into the village was surprisingly uneventful for one made under virtually no control. By the church, he slowed to about 40 m.p.h. and decided to take the turning whch led up the hill, over the Quantocks to Nether Stowey.

It was pure intuition and it was a blind corner. He took it at 30 m.p.h. and then applied the brakes as fast as he could, but, alas, too late. He was conscious of the unpleasant crunch of an animal on the radiator grille, also of a horse rearing immediately in front of him. He swerved, just missed the horse and ended up at right angles across the road.

'It's the bloody hunt,' moaned Grithbrice. Bognor opened his eyes expecting the worst and saw it. A few feet away lay a very dead-looking brown and white hound. Just beside it a figure in hunting pink was staggering about holding his hands to his head, and a little further away a riderless horse was running noisily and dangerously amok. All around more hounds bayed and red-faced horsemen and women waved whips and crops and shouted to one another. As he sat dazed in front of the wheel he saw a boot-faced woman dismount and walk towards them brandishing a riding crop. He didn't like the way things were moving. The boot-faced matron banged on the window and he rolled it down.

'I'm the Master here,' she bawled at him, showing all the fillings in her teeth. 'What in God's name do you think you're doing?'

'Have you see a green Lagonda?'

'I'll say we have. It was Basil Lydeard and he said he was being chased by two murdering ...' Her already thunderous expression darkened further and for an instant Bognor thought she was about to strike him. 'By God,' she shrieked, and turned to address her fellow hunters. 'By God,' she screamed again. 'It's those bloody poachers after Basil Lydeard. Let's have them out!'

One or two of the men started to dismount but, before they could, Bognor slipped the clutch in, turned the wheel sharply and put his foot down. He had the momentary but considerable satisfaction of seeing the look of fury on the Master's face as she was hurled sideways into the ditch, and then he was away, with the Mini screeching in protest as he accelerated up a gradient of one in four.

'Can a horse go as fast as a car?' he asked desperately.

'Across country, yes,' sighed Grithbrice.

'Shit,' said Bognor, as the little car struggled on. Suddenly as they went round the corner, they saw the Lagonda. It was less than half a mile ahead and smoking dangerously.

'We should get him now,' said Bognor exultantly. He pressed his foot as hard as it would go and managed to coax the car up to a protesting 30 m.p.h. In front of them the Lagonda, belching clouds of black fumes, was climbing at no more than 25. It was a two-snail race.

At the top of the hill they had almost caught him, but to Bognor's surprise and horror the Marquis swung his old machine hard to the right and shot off along a rough dirt track.

'Christ,' said Bognor. 'We're going to have to go across country.'

'No alternative,' said Grithbrice feebly, and a few seconds later they were jolting over the heavily rutted path on the spine of the Quantocks. At first the Lagonda with its bigger wheels and high carriage pulled away from them, while Bognor fought to keep the little Mini moving. But gradually Bognor's increasing skill and Lydeard's worsening engine trouble combined to reduce the deficit, until they were almost together.

'Hold tight,' said Bognor, 'I'm going alongside. Tell him not to be a bloody fool and make him stop.' So saying, he put his foot down until the Mini was bucking along the hillside at more than 40 m.p.h. carving a manic passage through heather and wortleberry bushes. 'Now!' he shouted, as he glanced across and saw Basil Lydeard almost exactly alongside. His face was vivid purple and his bulging eyes looked straight ahead as he gripped the steering wheel with rigid arms. Bognor was irresistibly reminded of Mr Toad in *The Wind in the Willows*. 'Now,' he shouted again, and watched Grithbrice lean out and gesture imploringly. It had no effect whatever.

'I'm going to ram him,' screamed Bognor. 'Hold on.' But just as he was about to swing the wheel hard to the left he saw a barbed wire fence rushing towards them. He braked just in time, and watched in despair as the Lagonda sped through a gateway and accelerated over a

273

track which had suddenly changed from mud to tarmac.

'We're going to lose him,' said Bognor. He reversed and followed, but Lydeard's lead had increased. The improving road now ran steeply downhill and the Lagonda was racing down it, although the smoke and fumes had not diminished at all. Bognor realized that Lydeard must have switched off the engine and was coasting.

Half a mile on, the road widened and was straighter as it crossed another road before descending even more sharply towards the village of Cothelstone. The two men watched in horror as the fuming Lagonda hurtled over the crossroads and down the hill beyond.

'My God,' shouted Bognor. 'He can't have seen that lorry. He'll never make it.'

The lorry, an old-fashioned horsebox, was making heavy weather of the hill, grinding upwards at walking pace. The driver had no chance of manœuvring at all, and Lydeard for his part was virtually out of control. From where Bognor and Grithbrice watched, it seemed there must be a head-on collision, but at the last second Lydeard must have appreciated the danger because the Lagonda suddenly juddered to the right. There was a puff of smoke from the tyres as they failed to grip the surface; then a rending noise as the massive green vehicle ripped through the wooden fencing at the roadside and leapt into the air.

It hung there for an instant and then bounced three times before it came to rest at the bottom of the slope in a field yellow with buttercups. Bognor noticed one of the wheels still spinning crazily and watched, mesmerized, as a thin snake of flame stretched out from the wreck. A second later there was a dull explosion as the flame reached the petrol tank and Bognor winced.

'Last of the Lydeards,' he said flatly.

★   ★   ★

That evening he and Monica had a muted dinner at the Basil Street Hotel. 'The zoo,' she said, after listening to his account, 'said that bison are renowned for their sense of smell.'

★   ★   ★

Next day he presented his report to Parkinson and watched as he read it. After an attentive perusal his boss gave him one of his old-fashioned looks. 'Before you start feeling pleased with yourself, read this,' he said.

The telegram said: 'Outraged appalled latest Grithbrice crime. Proceeding south soonest prevent more carnage. McCrum.'

'Oh, my God,' said Bognor.